THE MURPHY STORIES

MARK COSTELLO

The
Murphy
Stories

UNIVERSITY OF ILLINOIS PRESS

Urbana, Chicago, London

Acknowledgments: *Chicago Review,* "Punch & Judy"; *Epoch,* "Strong Is Your Hold O Love"; *Transatlantic Review,* "Murphy Agonistes" and "Murphy's Xmas"; *North American Review,* "Murphy in Missouri." "Murphy's Xmas" was reprinted in *The Best American Short Stories: 1969,* ed. Martha Foley and David Burnett, Houghton Mifflin Co., Boston, 1969.

TERESA

Callahan's Black Cadillacs

UNCLE MORT

Out of World War II he swings, fat, flatulent, hemorrhoidal, hyperbolic, sleepy, lazy, squat, penniless, hypertense. My sense of him is dazzled, Pauline, hysterical. Looming before me, he yawns, stretches, thumps me on the head. God is dead, he says and falls back on his bed. His bed is broad, sour, universal, uterine, vertiginous, pitiless, plenary, profound. He sleeps in attics, basements, hallways, hammocks, tree houses, parks, coal bins, beer trucks, movie houses and in the back of Singer Sewing Machine trucks. Yawning and slamming the door of a Singer Sewing Machine truck, he curls up in the back of it, his sleep a glue in which he rocks jobless, comatose and fugitive, waking in the middle of the afternoon to halitosis, pyorrhea, dandruff, psoriasis, ringworm, anal itch, all of the diseases of sloth, escape, immobility, his sleep a funk, a gunk of which my scolding, optimistic mother would love to cleanse him. Wake up, wake up, she whispers in his hairy ear, wash your face, scrub your teeth, take a bath, shampoo your hair, shave, clip your nails, powder your feet, shine your shoes, change your clothes, get up, get going, look alive boy, look alive!

More dead than alive, he sighs, looks at her, smiles, belches, farts, scratches, stretches, yawns and falls back to sleep, his sleep moving him from house to house, from relative to relative, from aunt to uncle to cousin then back again, his sleep wearing a raw, crusty slot in the family's mattresses and beds, my mother and father rousing him endlessly out of bed, all of my aunts, uncles and cousins scolding, nagging, cursing and upbraiding him, trying to make him bathe, work, wake up and for Christ's sake behave for a change like a decent man.

Manly, huge, indecent, enraged, he wakes to the scream of a telephone my hopeful mother has chosen to let ring. It is an old and characteristic trick, but it takes him as always by surprise. Rising from the sofa, he opens his eyes, pinches his nose, lets rip a coronary and horrible fart. Bending forward at the waist, he begins to curse and clutch his chest, his mouth opening and closing as if his heart had been ripped loose by his fart, as if it were beating now upon his tongue, his hands fumbling in his pockets and below his belt, the phone ringing somewhere in his guts, a black and electric alarm connected clearly to the dread itch and tingle of his single hemorrhoid, some dim, dumb, dreary, cast-iron little job in a munitions plant or county courthouse, a grimy grenade about to go off in the ass of his ease, killing not only himself but all the family with him, blowing wan and nervous uncles to jellied smithereens, blasting wedding rings and rosary beads from the upraised hands of castigating aunts, self-righteous cousins.

Raising both hands above his head, he says *all right, all right,* and rises from the sofa. His breadth and bulk stir the air, send a stink across the room, a pissy, angry scent of lion, tiger, snake, ape, extinction; the polar bear, the grizzly bear, the giant three-toed sloth lurching and crashing across the living room, erasing itself against urn, furniture, knickknack stand; a hackled, hang-dog, hog-tied hulk knocking the phone to the floor and placing a heavy hand across the receiver, taking a deep breath and beginning now to lie, to deny not only his existence but his posterity, the big, warm, dogged family that will not leave him alone, that keeps calling and calling, offering over and over the penultimate

2

job to which any man in his right mind, no matter how god damned sleazy lazy he is, will have finally by god to answer yes.

But he says no. And he says it with a desperation that darkens the dark of the corner in which he kneels. He whispers no, no, no, and one hears cage doors slamming, prayer wheels spinning, urine draining. He says never, never never, and the word becomes a zoo, a monastery in which he kneels among armadillos, goats, bulldogs, possums; bowed negative shapes that shape his refusals with armor plate, horns, fangs, fakery, procrastination.

Coughing a deep, procrastinatory cough, he clears his throat and refuses jobs with the park board, school board, parole board, draft board, board of health, welfare and education, liquor commission, highway commission, watershed planning commission; everywhere he turns, new jobs are opening up for him, soft wide jobs that sink him to the hip in worry and haste; well-paying political jobs that hold him in a paste of favors, dollars, apology. He says no, no, no, but his refusals are too terse, too perspirate; I can tell by the way he begins to itch and scratch that he feels trapped, that he is up against it, that he is talking now to my calm, kind, accommodating father. Who's calling as always from his glassed-in office in the State Employment Office.

Where, from 8 to 5 each day, he weaves amid the coat racks and the potted plants, knitting his brows and gnashing his teeth, tracking down jobs in convents, hatchet factories, junk yards, coal yards and Singer Sewing Machine trucks, my father filling every empty space in our town with jobs, stuffing cash and hard-earned money into the darkest, most unlikely pits and corners of our town, his job turning him now toward his own home and family, a thick, fat pocket of joblessness that hisses and thrashes in the darkest corner of his own darkened living room, a joblessness that he cannot touch or expunge, a fecklessness that will never soften or flower, bursting neither today nor tomorrow nor

3

the next day into a shrub of money, cash, salary, any greener, cleaner, more American way of life.

Death, death, death, a voice whispers, you're trying to put me to death. Then the phone comes crashing down and out of the hooks and folds of wool and brass a bottle rises, tips, begins to gurgle and drain. It is a familiar sound, a sound of wine, ammonia, blame.

Your father, a voice says, that was your father on the phone.

I know, I say, and it says, no you don't, you don't know a god damned thing.

In the cling of the lips to the bottle there is a smack and suck I've heard before. It is a semiannual sound. About twice a year the figure in the corner begins to writhe and curse and drink yellow wine. I think of dungeons and dipsomania; it is as if many pairs of pants have been pissed and stuffed into all the windows of the room; that atmosphere goes black then turns back upon itself, the voice in the corner murmurs words of sulphur, repetition, pain. This family, it says, this fucking god damned family. Then the metaphor turns medieval. My father's jobs are shit, teeth, cancers, contusions, fingers, boils, hoofs, nails, donkeys, hatchets, bellows driven up the assholes of white chickens blown to feathery bits.

Bit by bit a politics begins to form. In the ammoniac reek and dark my father becomes a monster, a well-meaning vulgarian whose jobs kill and maim, whose state will never provide for its poor, its disaffiliated, its sick and its fanatic. Assuming a saintly, sick, fanatic tone, the voice begins to intone the names of Marx, Nietzsche, Norman Thomas, W. C. Fields, banging on the floor and calling now for light, moaning over and over again, where's all the light in this god damned world.

I snap on the light, and the light blurs, burns, whitens and divides. Squinting my eyes, I look at the figure in the corner and think of soap and fire, kerosene and naptha, all of the uniforms of World War II, which, filthy beyond washing, were probably put to flame. Somehow the barbers would have gotten the job. And they would have done it in flat fields just outside Paris on overcast days. I look at the figure in the corner and see thousands of bald-headed barbers standing before thousands of bonfires. Inside the flames there are coils of wool and filth and yellow linen, heaps of hair and whisker and dirty brass, piles of shoes and boots with broken soles, the figure in the corner beginning now to rise and moan, to show for the thousandth time, the design and dementia of his dress.

Dressed as always in the blacks and khakis of the U.S. Army, he wears a huge woolen overcoat with a woolen stocking cap crushed down on his balding head. He is only 26 years old, but already the capillaries have begun to open and break like black fleurs-de-lis in his cheeks and across his nose. His nose is rose, bulbous, profoundly pocked. In the pockets of his overcoat he carries a smattering of cash, chickenshit and broken cognac bottles. There is something European in his look. In the scent of his skin and the mud of his boots, there is a suggestion of Paris and Pilsen; bombed, barbed, liberated cities where the breweries have been blitzed and the beer is running in the gutters, the GIs on their knees in the gutters lapping up beer, rising with live chickens under their arms, their pockets filled with chickenshit and fresh eggs, all of them looking for poker games and piano players with burnt, stiffened fingers, Pilsen and Piccadilly girls who will fuck standing up, who will send them back to Central Illinois clapped up and disaffected; fat, remote, romantic figures who cannot adjust, who cannot stand the ornaments and the emblems of the homes to which they have been returned, who berate each item, every idiosyncrasy, the figure in the corner beginning now to mumble and curse at my father's elephant collection, all these blue-balled beasts of burden, the voice whispers, all these god damned killer fucking elephants.

5

There are, it's true, a lot of elephants. In all the doors and on all the desks, in all the corners and closets and under all the beds, there are elephants. It's my father who collects them. An ex-alcoholic with a broken nose and sour stomach, he celebrates his debt to the Republican Party with elephants. At night in winter he will sit on the sofa sipping milk and unwrapping lead elephants. He will pass them on to me and they will be heavy in my hands. My father will say, isn't this one a beauty, and I will hold it up before me, the rounded belly of the elephant sending waves of weight and security through my forearms, the two of us touching its trunk and beautiful tusks, my whole sense of our government depending on heavy majestic elephants doing all the work in distant Washington, D.C., pushing the legislation through Congress as they might push great fallen sawed-up trunks of teakwood through the jungles of Ceylon, my father and I waiting for Mom to come home from the Saint Elizabeth Sodality meeting, the three of us saying the rosary together in the living room, praying for the conversion of Russia amid tissue paper and newly unwrapped lead elephants, the walls lined with framed replicas of Christ and Eisenhower, our prayers rising now against the angers and claustrophobias of the figure in the corner whispering oppressive, oppressive, oppressive, I can't stand this fucking air anymore, I'm leaving town and never coming back.

I look at him and he says you don't believe me do you.

I say yes and he says no you don't, tipping up his bottle of wine and beginning now to button the broken buttons of his overcoat.

They can take their dumb, debilitating jobs, he says, and stick them.

As he says this, he sticks a thumb in front of my face, motioning for me to pull it. I pull it and he lets rip a fart that rattles all the crucifixes and presidential pictures in the room. It is as if my father's elephants have chosen to fart on cue, clapping stale air from their great flapping assholes, the room smelling suddenly of shrapnel and hot lead. Again it is a wounded, coronary, over-violent atmosphere, one that calls for catgut, plasma, heart massage. With my heart in my mouth, I jump from my chair, run to my room and break open the belly of an elephant I keep hidden in the hot-air register. Cash falls out into my hand, quarters, dimes, pennies and green five-dollar bills.

Here, I tell him and hand over $15.72, you'll need this on the road.

Formal, sudden, loving, my gesture chokes him up.

You little fucker, he says, you little son of a bitch how much is here?

$15.72.

Looking down at me, he places a hand upon my head. Formal, slow, paternal, the pressure of his gesture almost puts me to my knees.

So long, he says, and messes up my hair, I'll see you in the funny papers.

THE FUNNY PAPERS

At night in winter, my aunt worries about the color of her hair. Her name is Hatt and her hair is a fried, manufactured black. My mother does this to her. On cold Monday nights in February Aunt Hatt sits at the kitchen table with white towels over her shoulders, metallic spinwheels and pins in her hair. The table is filled with white crockery filled with black dye. Her hands protected by white rubber gloves, my mother dips white cotton balls in the black dye and daubs it to Aunt Hatt's hair. In the air there is a scent of navy beans from supper and Aunt Hatt issues the warning she issues each time my mother dyes her hair. Don't get it too black, she says, don't get it too black. Don't worry, my mother daubs and promises, I won't get it too black,

when it is too black already, when it was too black before my
mother ever started making it blacker, when nothing could ever
be as black as my Aunt Hatt's hair is black *Mack, Mack, Mack.*
It is not so much a name as it is a refrain. The sound Aunt
Hatt makes as my mother departs on the steaming train for
Chicago. *Mack, Mack, Mack,* the sound taps at the tanks and
tinkling machine guns of 1942, 3, 4, 5. This is World War II. On
all the sidewalks of our neighborhood, swastikas have been scrib-
bled with bits of orange brickbat. Today Mack is in Dover, Dun-
kirk, Brest, Paris, Pilsen. Tomorrow Mack will take shrapnel in
Normandy, Nantes, Wetzlar. Service Stars and Purple Hearts
turn brown in bay windows up and down the block. Kneeling before the kitchen stove, Aunt Hatt prays for Mack her GI and
Mack her nephew, Mack her doubt and Mack her worry.
Harried, wary, I crawl after supper through the hedges, bunkers,
black barbed wire of World War II. Calling my name from the
kitchen window, Aunt Hatt calls artillery down upon my head.
Hot, white, swastika-shaped, the shrapnel whines in my guts, in-
sists as always on its single sound. Whispering *Mack, Mack,*
Mack, Aunt Hatt puts me through my prayers and washing, leads
me at last to our big double bed.

Where neither of us sleeps. Because we have been left alone
these days. My father has taken a wartime job at a State Employment Office in Chicago and every Tuesday morning my
mother boards the Wabash "Banner Blue" to join him there. So
Aunt Hatt and I lie sleepless in bed, waiting for prowlers. And
they always come. In the form, each time, of Uncle Mort. Who
is almost too perfect for the purposes of Aunt Hatt's worry. It's
October, November, December and all over town the movies are
playing Frankenstein, Wolfman, Dracula. And Uncle Mort must
see them all. Slipping from the Empress to the Avon to the Al-
hambra, Uncle Mort takes his seat, as he always does, smack in
the center of the very first row. He's rapt, ravenous. His fat right

fist thrashes in a red, white and blue candy-striped bag of buttered popcorn, his big shoulders bend forward under the projectionist's white beam, his eyes fix dirty, meaty, protuberant and mean upon the silver screen. Now a bottle of yellow wine gurgles at his mouth and Uncle Mort's caught up in swirls of banshee wing and werewolf fang that bang each midnight against the side of our house.

Rising from the bed, Aunt Hatt hisses *what was that?*

Only Uncle Mort, I whisper, trying to scare us.

She is crouched at the window, shaking her head. No, she says, not this time it isn't. There's somebody out there, trying to get in.

Propped up on one elbow, I look at Aunt Hatt. She is old and she is thin. She is breathing fast. She wears a mauve nightgown, Christ's plastic heart stuck on a patch of purple felt pinned to a shoulder strap. Sitting up, I whisper it's only Uncle Mort out there Aunt Hatt, come on back to bed.

But she doesn't move. So I rise, throw back the covers, join her vigil at the window. The floor is cold, my spine chilled, I try my best to smile, be manly. Bending down, I peer in the direction of her pointed finger.

There's something down there at the other end of the house, she says, *squatting in the shrubs.* Pressing my nose against the glass, I catch a glimpse of Uncle Mort. His aspect, as he slips around the corner of the house, is insane, Frankensteinian. His face is pasty; around his guts and hips there is a girth that looks electrified, a fat made of magnetos that crackle, belch and slam now against the kitchen then the bathroom windows, Aunt Hatt hissing *what was that, what was that,* clutching her rosary beads and racing from room to room, window to window, Uncle Mort slapping and knocking against all the walls of the house at once, Aunt Hatt whispering *my God, my God,* our chase ending as it always does, in front of a telephone I can't let Aunt Hatt get to. Because if I do, she'll have all of my policeman uncles out here in an instant. Yellow and blue, their squad cars will tick at the curbs. Yellow-beamed, their flashlights will probe the shrubs, garage, attic, basement and coal bin, Aunt Hatt wanting to ask them, I know, to search for prowlers in the roaring furnace. Then clicking off their flashlights and shaking their heads, my policeman uncles will tell Aunt Hatt and me to go back to bed. Grinning, they'll slap me on shoulders that I now straighten against a sudden, yet expected silence in our house.

Come on, Aunt Hatt, I whisper, Uncle Mort's gone. Let's go back to bed and get some sleep.

But we don't. All night long we worry, pray, turn, toss, rise month after month at 6 A.M. to offer our mass and communion for *Mack, Mack, Mack,* gray days that take me to the sixth grade of St. Matt's School, Aunt Hatt just across the alley to St. Ann's Hospital. All day long the big blond smokestacks of St. Ann's Hospital belch black smoke. At 4:30 P.M., the palms of my hands pink and muddy from dribbling basketballs on icy asphalt after school, I go to pick up Aunt Hatt when she's done with work. She works in the basement of St. Ann's in the shipping and receiving room. Choosing one from a long line of ancient, high-backed wicker wheelchairs, I sit down amid steel cylinders of oxygen marked Danger No Smoking and wait. All around me are wood crates filled with big bottles of dextrose and glucose. Lit by red Exit signs, the dim, endless corridors are lined with packs of twisting, fat, gray pipes that tick and hiss along the ceiling. Aunt Hatt's office, too, is filled with valves and clanging pipes: with nuns, roses, boxes of Fanny May candies delivered to patients who could not eat them.

Ashen, harassed, Aunt Hatt always stands, never sits behind her desk. Her thin fingers flash, she impales invoices on a spike and the telephone rings. Her voice shakes, her veins are lilac. She says: *yes Mother Superior, no Mother Superior,* the nuns in heavy, white wool habits swishing in and out, making their thousand demands, calling her "Harriet," demeaning her spinsterhood with the clatter of rosary beads against their sisterly thick thighs.

At 5 P.M., when Aunt Hatt's supposed to get off work, the florists' trucks begin to arrive. Slow, friendly, their eyes out of focus and their faces pitted with acne, the 35-year-old brain-damaged sons of Irish florists from all over town descend into Aunt Hatt's office carrying vases of flowers wrapped in banners reading Get Well and Speedy Recovery. Smiling, Aunt Hatt offers them a piece of candy or two. For a moment they linger in her office talking about Lent and novenas. Devout, gray-headed, some of them have streaks of white in their eyelashes and eyebrows. As they speak about novenas and giving up candy for Lent, their eyelashes blink white and uncertain. Then they thank Aunt Hatt and leave. Their departures are thicker, slower and more mild than their arrivals. Looking down at me in my wheelchair, they stammer, stutter, speak my name. Then they close the door and Aunt Hatt calls them "God's bless'd." Sighing, she reaches for her coat. But she's too late. The nuns swish in to whisper *potatoes, plasma, peaches, crutches.* Aunt Hatt nods, trembles, picks up the phone. Over and over she apologizes as she serves me toasted cheese sandwiches, hard-boiled eggs, baked apples, pale donuts and cartons of chocolate milk from the hospital kitchen.

At 7 P.M., the cancer pad ladies arrive. They are a dozen strong. Glaucomatous, goitered, liver-spotted, ancient, the cancer pad ladies work five nights a week, for free, in a brightly lit little room just down the corridor from Aunt Hatt's office in the basement of St. Ann's. Out of napkins, doilies, pillowcases and old white shirts, they fashion pads to be placed below the bedding of suppurating cancer patients on St. Ann's warm fourth floor. Often I wheel my wheelchair down the corridor and look in at them. Each one wears a black pillbox hat upon her head and their eyeglasses glint, their needles glitter. Sitting rigid in their chairs, the cancer pad ladies chatter on and on about signs of cancer in warts, moles, corns, bones, lips, breasts, the peculiar scent of cancer in certain cancer patients' stools. And though they sometimes may discuss a death by stroke or rupture of the spleen, their conversation always loops back to its single center. Cancer, cancer, cancer.

At 7:45 P.M., Aunt Hatt finally slips on her coat. But now as she reaches down her hand to me, she draws me up and out of my wheelchair into a new and cruel curiosity about cancer. Which Aunt Hatt fears, I know, in her warts, moles, breasts, bones, corns, lips, stools. And which, according to Uncle Mort, seeps from the very furnaces and big blond smokestacks of St. Ann's Hospital. *Every night,* he whispers, *they bring down the arms, tits and legs they cut off on the operating table, burn them in the furnace and if you sniff the smoke from the chimneys, you can get cancer too.* Deep in a flame of crates, bedsheets, cancer pads, gauze and roses, the bones and breasts begin to fry. Breathing soot from the chimneys of St. Ann's, I cough against a need to tease and pester Aunt Hatt with Uncle Mort's lie. But I keep quiet and she takes my hand, beginning as she does so to hum "Molly Malone." Which is a warning of sorts. Because each time Aunt Hatt takes my hand and begins to hum "Molly Malone," she begins at the same time to have trouble with her heart. Tonight is no exception. Out of the corner of my eye, I watch her. The wings of her nostrils flare, she squeezes my hand. Let's stop here for a second, she says, and catch our breath. Holding my breath, I watch Aunt Hatt's breath fly out of her mouth. Her heart trouble has delivered us, as it always delivers us, onto the steps in front of St. Matt's Church. Pigeons flap their wings and Aunt Hatt gasps. Looking right and left, I squeeze her hand and ask if she's all right. Her chest heaves, her eyes dilate, I turn to see if anybody is watching. Breathing through my mouth, I step between her and the wind off the chimneys of St. Ann's. Beginning once more to hum "Molly Malone," she looks up at the big double doors of St. Matt's Church: let's just step inside, she whispers, I'll take a heart pill and we'll warm our hands. It is not a pause, it is a pilgrimage, retreat, complete ordeal. For a full two hours we work the church for all it's worth. Dipping our fingers in the icy holy water fount, we move past black Gothic confessional boxes to the altars of St. Joseph and Our Lady of Perpetual Help. Stopping to drop coins into loud steel strongboxes, we light first the lilac, then the red votive lights. Kneeling at the communion rail, we strike our breasts. Rising, we genuflect, kneel, pray, move up and down the aisles through all twelve stations of the cross. As I follow her, I watch Aunt Hatt. Her jaws grind, her false teeth clack. Kneeling on the cold linoleum, staring up at Christ scourged, spat upon and crucified, she beats her breast and prays so hard it is as if at any moment her prayers are going to begin to work up a froth. Listening to the creak of Aunt Hatt's knees, I see her as a zealot, some wild Irish lady who cleans, scours and scalds the church with her prayers, great buckets and scrub brushes clanging in the dark. Arriving finally at the last row at the back of the church, Aunt Hatt and I kneel now and begin to pray in earnest for *Mack, Mack, Mack.* Flickering, the votive lights throw Aunt Hatt's profile delicate and spatulate against the stained-glass windows. Spinning outward, Aunt Hatt's prayers seem to swarm and thicken, lead us into January, February, March, April, the dim and dreary time of Uncle Mort's hibernation.

He does this about twice a year. Goes to sleep and sleeps in the direction of the city limits. Moving from my father's to my mother's bed, he sleeps outward through the cots, divans, hammocks and gliders of more and more distant relatives, sleeping on and on until we're sure he's slept himself right out of town, Aunt Hatt certain that he's gone off finally to settle down, to take the job she's always dreamed he'd take. But I know different.

It's a slow time for me. Aunt Hatt's working late these after-noons and often I find myself about 4:30 or 5 o'clock walking the Wabash tracks north, in the direction of Chicago. Head bowed and shoulders hunched, I'm moving, I know, toward our foul town dump. The day is gray and snowless; pigeons burst white through the yellow smoke of St. Ann's Hospital, wheel high against the tar-marked grain elevators that loom on the edges of our neighborhood. Through the shadow and smoke, the tracks look Appian, Damascan, dolorous. Bells toll and clang, whistles whiten and scream. Breathing in the heavy steam of the soybean mills on the edge of town, I seem to exhale comic strips, deadly coils of comedy that fell and locate Uncle Mort in a snarl of garbage, the Wabash tracks leading me down now to the land of the Sunday funnies, the orange and yellow hell of our foul town dump.

Where, amid burnt-out mattresses and glutted gliders, I con-sider the conditions of Uncle Mort's sleep. This is the perfect place, the perfect time of day and year. In the air there is a scent of dream and dynamite, a soughing of feathers, nitroglycerine and drool. Sitting down on the cold end of a smoking sofa, I pic-ture Uncle Mort curled up deep in the heart of the dump, buried by bulldozers in a cocoon of eggshell, albumen, excelsior and grease, his sleep untouched by the worry of Aunt Hatt or any of his other relatives. Then I look up, and all over the dump Sun-day funnies are rising and blowing, dreamy orange and yellow sheets full of bullets, badges, brickbats, billy clubs: soon pigs belonging to my aunts and uncles will be released from Park Board pens and trucks to scream and circle in our foul town dump, bald park policemen paid off by my aunts and uncles de-scending to beat and gather the pigs, to clear a space in which, closing my eyes to the ribs and spines of pigs, I turn homeward and know now that our house is filling with Singer Sewing Machines.

This, too, happens about twice a year. Our house begins to fill with Singer Sewing Machines. It's all the company's fault. Because twice a year, every year, no matter how much he has bilked, insulted, disappointed and cost them in the past, the Singer Sewing Machine Company gives Uncle Mort a job selling Singer Sewing Machines. This time's just like last. When I get home, Aunt Hatt has already returned from work, is opening the kitchen door, ready to answer the first question that she knows I'll ask: *is he back?*

Yes.

Working?

Yes.

Singer Sewing Machine?

Yes.

Drunk?

Sober.

Dirty?

Clean.

The house fills, as she says this, with song and steam. Harsh, false, Middle European, the sounds I hear are the sounds I hear each time Uncle Mort takes his biannual bath. Huffing, grunting, scrubbing, Uncle Mort talks in tongues, fills the air with *k*'s and *ski*'s, a crazy Polish whisper that litters our sidewalks with broken wine bottles, the shattered signs of a pledge that flecks our bathtub with pubic hair and toenail clippings, coils of ocher underwear quivering and stiffening upon the bathroom floor: *he must have left,* Aunt Hatt says, *about an hour ago.*

How do you know?

When I was getting off work, she says, I saw the truck.

The Singer Sewing Machine truck?

Yes.

Where?

Turning the corner, she says, heading uptown.

I look down and Aunt Hatt is, as always, wringing her hands. And telling me for the thousandth time that she is *sick,* absolutely worried *sick* about all these sewing machines, leading me as she does past stack after stack of Singer Sewing Machines piled in every corner of every bedroom in the house, Aunt Hatt touching my arm and asking at last *what's he ever going to do with all these expensive, expensive sewing machines?*

The answer, of course, is nothing. Because Uncle Mort has risen from our bathtub in the shape of a clipped, trimmed, sparkling, polished, grinning, bald-headed, red-nosed seller of Singer Sewing Machines who sells no Singer Sewing Machines, who drops them off instead for trial. *Here, take this on trial,* he says, *and see if you don't by god fall in love with it,* nobody ever trying it and nobody ever falling in love with it, our closets filling higher and higher with new, unused Singer Sewing Machines, Uncle Mort never returning to sell or claim his Singer Sewing Machines, the people from Singer Sewing Machine finally showing up one day to take back their sewing machines and to inquire about their truck, their search leading them as it must to our foul town dump, a trough of ice, sleep, slime, feather and flaming grease into which Uncle Mort dives again and again, a furry, oily, loon-like shadow flickering downward against Aunt Hatt's *Mack, Mack, Mack,* Uncle Mort bursting after about three weeks through tin can, tarp and fiery bedstead, asking as always the single question for which Aunt Hatt can never find an answer: *how about a little feel, how about a little feel?*

It's less a request for breast than money. Blood money. Money that Uncle Mort seems to pull not from Aunt Hatt's purse but chest, Uncle Mort driving his fat fist through the black patent leather of her purse into her ribcage, extracting between the years of 1942 and 1945 over two thousand dark, jagged dollars every penny of which, I know, will go unpaid. And Aunt Hatt knows it too. Because even before Uncle Mort arrives at our house, even

before he slams through the door and asks her for *a little feel,*
Aunt Hatt reaches for her purse, raises it to her withered, in-
dented chest, begins to recite to me the long list of her war-year
loans to Uncle Mort, vowing as she does so not to give him, *so
help me,* another red cent, Aunt Hatt rising now from the supper
table, preparing as always to hide her money.

But she's too late. Even before she can pass the stove and refrigerator, Uncle Mort's through the door, hovering over her,
asking for *a little feel, a little feel.* It's an old routine, an ancient
chase. Loud, rattling, it takes them through every room in the
house. With him Uncle Mort brings a scent of grease, piss, fuel
oil, yellow wine, his snout and mouth darkened by oil drums and
truck tires burning blackly in our foul town dump. Black, im-
pacted, his fingernails dribble graphite and charcoal as he grinds
them in front of Aunt Hatt's breasts. His question is slurred, incessant. *How about a little feel, how about a little feel?* But that's
not what he wants. He wants a pinch. And Aunt Hatt knows it.
Turning, she warns Uncle Mort about cancer of the breast, about
how, if he pinches her, he can give her cancer of the breast. It's
a warning that backs her each time into the tightest corner of
our little living room, Uncle Mort raising his arms and closing
in, Aunt Hatt's pleas and warnings ending with a flashing of cash
and a slamming of doors, Uncle Mort slamming out the front
door and Aunt Hatt slamming her hand down on the kitchen
table. Staring at me, she whispers: *$15.72! I gave him $15.72!*
You know, don't you, what he's going to do with that money?

No.

Yes you do.

No I don't.

Guess.

Aunt Hatt's dress is blue and I say *buy a bus ticket.*

She says *ha* and I say *train ticket.*

She says *whew* I say *food* and she says *food my foot!*

Then she stamps her foot and though I am still sitting in my chair, we seem to go into a dance, waltz, mint blue tango. Bending over me, Aunt Hatt whispers *booze, booze, booze,* he's going to buy *booze* with that $15.72 and I knew it when I gave it to him didn't I? Then she's marching bang, bang, bang, down the basement stairs, Aunt Hatt's punishment made up somehow of her own terrible descension of the stairs, her feet beating silver and numerical against their surfaces, her rage taking her to the small shrine she's fixed up with orange crates and votive lights at the far end of the basement, Aunt Hatt's prayers for *Mack, Mack, Mack,* grinding on and on until they conclude at last in V-E Day, the wonderful afternoon, nine months later, of Mack's homecoming.

Which is no homecoming at all. Because it's over before it begins. Stepping off the Wabash "Banner Blue" with his blond war bride on his arm, Mack's in no mood for family, friends or talk, he's interested instead in our New Used Car lots. Where, moving through a heavy January snow, he kicks tires, pumps brakes, peers below the hoods of a hundred cars before he chooses finally a rusty Hudson that he fills with white suitcases, huge hatboxes, coolers full of German beer, Wisconsin cheese. Grinning and waving, Mack honks the horn of his rusty Hudson, takes off with his blond war bride in the direction of sunny San Diego, the ton of money he's going to make in TV sales and TV service, Mack leaving Aunt Hatt with a quick kiss on the cheek, me with a bag of shrapnel, blood-stained leather, sour souvenirs.

It's strange stuff. All of it is German and all of it is blood-stained. Late in the afternoon of Mack's departure, I sit down and examine it. With the light failing and Aunt Hatt kneeling in front of her basement shrine praying for Mack's success out in sunny San Diego, I squat on the living room floor, lift a German paratrooper's helmet above me, peer up at the black blood stains on its leather straps. Then I set the helmet down on my head and three years pass. Praying for *Mack, Mack, Mack,* out in sunny San Diego, Aunt Hatt grows thin in Central Illinois. From below the lace of her hat and from out of the fur of her collar comes a tarnished, acrid, metallic scent. Bent forward against the wind, she moves from home to church to work, in a halting, embarrassed pattern designed to avoid my father. He's back from his wartime job in Chicago now, and Aunt Hatt's taken an apartment of her own.

Usually it's about 6 P.M. and the sparrows are loud on the telephone lines outside the kitchen window. Stopping off only long enough to catch her breath, Aunt Hatt asks when my father's going to be home for supper. Refusing my mother's offer of dinner or at least a cup of tea, Aunt Hatt takes a heart pill and worries about Mack, whose TV business in San Diego is huge, wavering and growing, about Uncle Mort, who keeps pestering her for money, about the headlights of my father's car, which will flash at any moment now on the doors of our tilted garage. When she stands and peers this way from our kitchen window, Aunt Hatt's exhaustion shows most clearly along her jaw, her false teeth set farther forward on her jaw than they have ever been before. Then she begins to grind her teeth and I feel once more the fit of a German paratrooper's helmet on my head, imagine Aunt Hatt's lips turning blue beneath its weight, her black hair sticking stiff from below its steel rim, Aunt Hatt stumbling up from the basement of St. Ann's with a German paratrooper's helmet on her head, the stains on its straps darkening her throat and shortening her breath, Aunt Hatt's prayers turning to a froth at the edges of her mouth, the headlights of my father's car flashing one January evening on Aunt Hatt's stricken profile, the gasps and sputterings of her single, final heart attack.

Sometimes up dilapidated alleyways, past garages wrapped in

raw morning-glory vines, Uncle Mort and I have moved in a haze
of lies; Uncle Mort sipping yellow wine and lying to me about
machine guns, grenades, trip flares, pig stickers, lugers and bronze
stars, lies that he murmurs like a breviary, lies that he expects
me less to believe than to memorize, both of us knowing full well
that he never saw combat, that he never even got out of the
States, that he was released with high blood pressure after spend-
ing less than three weeks in February 1942 in a supply dump in
the Quartermaster Corps in Fort Riley, Kansas, Uncle Mort going on and on until the walking and the lying make him thirsty,
lead him off toward Aunt Hatt, the invariable chase for *a little
feel,* all of his lies buzzing now around her heart attack and hos-
pitalization, her steady, heaving decline, a time when at last he
wants to tell the truth. Which he works at like a butcher.

I'm standing at the kitchen window and he's standing right
beside me. In his fat right fist, he holds a bottle of yellow wine.
He tips it up and the lies chop, hack, beat around my head. For
two weeks now he's been at it. Drinking yellow wine and lying
to me: catching me in the toilet at St. Ann's Hospital, cornering
me in the hallway near the statue of the Sacred Heart, his lies
whining hot around my head, Uncle Mort no longer lying to me
about pig stickers, lugers and bronze stars, but about Aunt Hatt.

Who moans in her bed while Uncle Mort whispers to me in
our kitchen. Standing at the window, I imagine her in the intensive care unit at St. Ann's. She is folded over on herself,
curled tight upon her side. From her nostrils and wrists, plastic
tubes loop upward above her head. Uncle Mort calls her *that
poor woman* and Aunt Hatt seems to jerk and stiffen in her bed.
He whispers *if you only knew* and the votive lights leap lilac and
red below the statue of the Sacred Heart. Then Uncle Mort puts
a hand on my shoulder, breathes, heaves, sweats, sighs; tries again
and again to tell me what he has to tell me before Aunt Hatt
dies.

And when he finally tells me, Uncle Mort stuns me; his words seem to move me across the kitchen, out the door, down the Wabash tracks in the direction of our foul town dump. The day is gray, my eyes glazed. As I drift by degrees through weeds and blowing Sunday funnies, I feel hollow, shallow, very guilty, desecrating with each step I step the car that must be buried, I know, somewhere in the trash below my feet. Looking out the kitchen window, I imagine it. Smashed, fractured, phosphorescent, it glows with age and bathtub gin, its back seat stained by Aunt Hatt's big mistake, the one she made, *by god* just like the rest of us. To the thrum and rumble of Uncle Mort's words, I close my eyes against a scent of carbon and charcoal, cough loud against the screech of car door opening then slamming shut deep inside our foul town dump. Looking down, I imagine Aunt Hatt hiding in the back seat of a black and flattened Ford buried a hundred feet below our foul town dump. It's a Model A or T, and its spiked wheels are crushed and jagged as ice picks. Now the back seat begins to throb. Dropping oily and loonlike through the trash toward Aunt Hatt, Uncle Mort smashes his fist through the glass. Reaching in not after a purse but a birth, Uncle Mort extracts not cash from Aunt Hatt, but a baby from Aunt Hatt. Hushed and hissing, the delivery is attended by neither father nor husband, blessed by neither matrimony nor Holy Mother Church. Calling Aunt Hatt an *unwed mother,* Uncle Mort reaches out, taps at my chest, asks now the last question he must ask me before she dies: and do you know, he whispers, when Mack will find out Hatt's his real mother?

I shake my head and he screams when it's *too late,* that's when. He won't find out, god damn it, *until that poor woman's dead!*

When he says this, he slams a fist down on the windowsill and Aunt Hatt dies, Uncle Mort making his proclamation and the phone ringing at the same time, my mother calling from the hospital to tell us that, God Rest Her Soul, Aunt Hatt is dead.

Often, often, we bear it away, the family flesh in Callahan's black Cadillacs. And though each funeral's vivid and particular in its rouges and in its roses, I have trouble sometimes sorting them out, cannot ever tell quite which is which. Again and again we leave St. Matt's Church bearing Aunt Hatt's tiny corpse, only to arrive at Calvary Cemetery with the ten-ton corpse of Uncle Mort. Under the weight of his big bronze box, my carbuncular uncles heave and redden while Uncle Mort farts loudly, sitting alone with me in a big black Cadillac, Aunt Hatt's funeral procession twisting and circling along one-way, fenced-in streets, under viaducts near the soybean mills, past lot after lot of New Used Cars.

Blind with sleep and smoking cigarettes, the workers from the soybean mills grind their teeth and grip their steering wheels. Tense, impatient, their faces float sallow in the squares they've scraped in the frost on their windshields. Matches flare, horns shriek. Twisting on the edge of his seat, Uncle Mort grins pale and nervous at each line of backed-up traffic that we pass. Elbowing me in the ribs, he whispers *just look at those miserable bastards, just look at them.* I look at them and three years pass. Through ashes, dust, frost and Dallas, Texas, Aunt Hatt's funeral procession loops outward in the direction of Uncle Mort's own death. *I'd rather be dead,* he whispers, *I'd rather be dead than shovel soybeans the rest of my god damned life,* that declaration somehow damning him to death in Dallas, Texas, somebody grinding an elbow into my ribs as I turn ever so slowly now toward the beaked and birdlike profile of Uncle Mort's orange-haired widow.

Scrunched between the shoulders of my uncles' thick, dark overcoats, she peers from the tinted windows of one of Callahan's black Cadillacs. Chattering on and on about how, during the last three years of his life, Uncle Mort settled down and straightened up, held a fine-paying job with Singer Sewing Machine there in Dallas, Texas, she warms to her real subject, returns again and again to the single, favorite theme of Aunt Hatt, Hatt, Hatt.

As our black Cadillacs move away from St. Matt's Church, Uncle Mort's widow tells us over and over about how, from the day she met him until the day he died, Uncle Mort talked and talked about Aunt Hatt, how devoted he was to her memory, how he had mass after mass said for the repose of poor Hatt's soul, how certain she was that Aunt Hatt had caused Uncle Mort's deathbed return to the Catholic Church. Then as we lurch over the cracked-up, corrugated streets of the soybean mills, Uncle Mort's widow begins to pull from her black patent leather purse picture postcard after picture postcard. Sighing and dabbing at her eyes with a black lace handkerchief, she tells us that she *just knew* we'd want to see these. And we do. My aunts and uncles ooh, ah, nod and sniffle as they pass the picture postcards back toward my corner of the Cadillac.

Shot from the air, the postcards show a big Veterans Hospital just outside Dallas, Texas. The shrubs are squat, the grass is hot. On the bright sidewalks and blond smokestacks of the Veterans Hospital, the shadow of a low-flying biplane seems to slur with the words By Air, Uncle Mort carefully addressing and stamping each postcard, but mailing none of them. On the back of the postcard bearing my mother's and father's address, Uncle Mort writes, *Lamb of God Who Takest Away the Sins of the World, Forgive Me.* And on each of the next nine Uncle Mort asks the Lamb of God or the Sacred Heart or the Holy Ghost or Christ Crucified to forgive him, ending every one with *mea culpa, mea culpa.* As I read his words, they seem scrawled in a more hurried and nervous hand, as if Uncle Mort were running a race against the very Cadillacs with which we now convey his corpse to Calvary Cemetery, trying to stop with his prayers and pleas, a funeral procession that takes us past, as it must, our foul town dump.

Closing my eyes, I see Uncle Mort weaving amid the glutted gliders and fiery bedsteads. A lead crucifix bangs against his chest and he falls face forward on a smoking sofa. Dressed in mint green gowns, army surgeons set to work at the base of his back. Nerve after nerve they sever to soothe him, but his blood pressure keeps rising. Under the knives and needles of the Veterans Hospital, a Model A or T throbs in the heart of our foul town dump as our black Cadillacs pass with a bump into Calvary Cemetery. And though we've been driving for what seems like hours, days, weeks, months, years, we're still not far from home.

Above the trees and tombstones, the chimneys of St. Ann's belch black smoke. From golden censers, dark sweet incense drifts. Dressed in lace, the priest moves across the frosted grass. Like the cancer pad ladies, he wears a black pillbox hat upon his head. Squat, ancient, clean-shaven and powerful through the gut, the priest lumbers up to the coffin. In his thick right fist he holds a hammer. He hacks the air and time and holy water stun all Satans with the single word *begone, begone.* As I look down at it, Uncle Mort's coffin seems to shudder and contract, to blur and blend with Aunt Hatt's coffin. Standing beside me on the frosted grass of Calvary Cemetery, Uncle Mort throws yet another elbow into my ribs, extracts from me now a last *god damn it* promise. *Whatever you do,* he says, *don't let them do this to me, don't let the sons of bitches sprinkle holy water on my god damned corpse.* Then the priest whispers *ashes to ashes, dust to dust,* the bulldozers whine higher in our foul town dump, a coffin thumps against the ground as now, for the final time, I lose Uncle Mort and Aunt Hatt to the hundred slamming doors of Callahan's black Cadillacs.

Punch & Judy

W<small>E</small> are searching this Sunday for negroes. The ones who loiter in lavender on curbs outside the Orlando Hotel. It's my father who's after them. It's his passion, profession. As he drives, he talks as always on a single subject. The subject of his job. Which is, as always, getting other people jobs. Especially negroes. According to my father there's not a negro in our town for whom, at one time or another, he hasn't gotten a job. And a good job too. Now as we pass the negroes standing in the sunlight on the white, white curbs, my father points at them. *I got him a job,* my father says, *and I got him a job too.* Every Sunday they are standing there, and every Sunday they salute. Rolling down the window, my father coughs and calls out their names. Opening their mouths and raising their pink palms in salute, the negroes grin and murmur as we pass them in our sleek state car.

A gas-eater and oil-burner, my father's sleek state car's a jet black 1944 Lincoln Zephyr with the state bird inscribed in gold on both its doors. In the trunk wrapped in immaculate rags there's row upon row of bright blue oil cans. Each time my father starts his sleek state car, he adds a can or two of oil, something addicted or medicinal about the glug-glug of the oil as it drains from the can, my father banging down the hood, an oily rush of air slamming into both our faces. How much daily oil my father's sleek state car requires, I cannot say. But the look he gives me tells me it's a secret between nobody but the two of us, a secret that he knows I'll keep. Now my father's sleek state car hacks, coughs, drifts jet black up the street. Behind us, blue coils of oil smoke billow from our twin exhausts. On both our doors, there's an identical deep gold inscription. For Official Use Only. Now as he talks to me, my father's talk seems official, humble, unimpeachable, our car and conversation somehow protected and directed by the inscriptions that we carry on our doors, our sleek state car squawking to a sudden, lurching and uncertain stop.

Painted across the pavement below our tires, there's a bright yellow, six-foot-long inscription that duplicates the inscription painted across both our doors. For Official Use Only. Parked now where we alone can park, smack in the shadow of the State Employment Office, my father and I endure together a moment of both privilege and uneasiness. It's curious, but his office is a place my father seems to come to only at night or on weekends. Now it's Sunday morning and as we enter it, my father does the one and only thing he does each time he visits his empty office. Leaving my side, he drifts off amid the typewriters and file cabinets. Lifting a set of rosary beads from his suitcoat pocket, he wraps them around his fist. Then he begins to weave from one end to the other of his office, a look of terrible concentration on his face, as if he were blessing or casing the place, memorizing its emptiness, his job getting other people jobs somehow dependent upon his knowledge of the arrangement of every pencil and each piece of furniture in the State Employment Office, coming up here each night and every weekend to *memorize, memorize, memorize,* my father's prayers and concentration leading us as they must toward my wedding day.

We are sitting in the backyard of our house. This is a reception. This is my sister's affair. The sun is shining and my father's elephant collection has spilled out of the house and onto the lawn. On all the tables and scattered at random on the burnt-out grass, little, leaden GOP elephants stand with their trunks raised, curled, trumpeting. The sun is hot and I sit in a plastic lawn chair, awaiting the favors of my father. When they fall, they fall heavy upon me. *Now that you're married son,* my father says and drops a hand upon my shoulder, *why don't you let me find you a good steady job.* Serene, steady, my father is moved somehow by his own offer. *I'd be only too happy to help you find something,* he adds and lowers his eyes, *after all that's my job you know.*

I know. I am 19 years old and for 19 years now my father's job has frightened me. My father's job is, as always, getting other people jobs. He is a Republican and I am out of work. He removes his hand from my shoulder and I shudder, shrink, see myself sitting at a desk in the State Employment Office. My job, too, is getting other people jobs. Framed replicas of Christ and Eisenhower hang on the walls above and behind my back. The hair on the back of my hands is thick with dust and evasion, my fingers tremble and blot the ink. Shifting among file cabinets and blond stenographers, my father pays a surprise visit to his office during working hours. Appearing at my side, he puts a hand upon my shoulder. *Unemployment,* he whispers, *is rising. There just aren't enough jobs to go around.* Then he is gone and I turn in my swivel chair to face the jobless. The jobless are legion. Stretching out in endless lines in front of my desk, the jobless work their gums, venetian blinds and American flags showing through the blank spaces in their mouths. In my stomach I am growing an ulcer. Every day I flatten it in the shape of the state bird. Promises beat notarized and rotten from my mouth. The State Employment Office fills with wings and ceiling fans. Beginning to moan and falter, their ribs curling like the ribs of poisoned dogs, the jobless writhe in feathery stacks on the floor of the State Employment Office, their cries driving me to rise now amid my father's sparkling garbage cans and leaden elephants, to put a hand on his shoulder, to drift off as I must toward Southern California.

Where my father's aorta breaks against bootsole, rifle stock, silken American flag. This is Southern California and I am in the U.S. Army. There are crows in the sky and the sergeants' mouths are open. Some of the sergeants have leukemia. Leukemia sings and gnaws below the brass insignia and khaki uniforms of certain sergeants who will weigh only 90 pounds when they die, a stylized strangulated cadence rising for the last time from their opened graves, the lids of their coffins slamming shut and my father clutching at his gut back in Central Illinois.

Soft landing, dark collapse. Dropping his razor, my father falls heavy to the bathroom floor. That's where, my sister whispers, she found him when she found him. Sitting there holding the toilet, white as a sheet, the shaving cream still on his face. And heavy, God was he heavy. Pressing the telephone to my head, I listen as my sister's voice lowers at midnight into a description of ambulance sirens and emergency rooms, her story concluding with a definition she speaks in tones both clinical and hushed. An aneurism, she whispers, is a pathological, blood-filled dilation of a blood vessel. Like a tiny balloon about to break in Dad's aorta. They spliced it, she tells me, with a piece of plastic tube. But my sister doesn't stop there. She provides now an image that gives me pause. Against the hospital windows, snow swirls and falls. Curled on his side, his penis, wrists and nostrils stuffed with plastic tubes, my father tries as best he can to say his rosary. But every few minutes or so he pauses long enough to speak my name, asking again and again when I'll be home from Southern California, his dry lips moving, calling for a shave.

Punch & Judy

A *shave*. It's not a plea, it's an honor. A man of many razors, clippers, pincers, scissors, colognes, salts, styptics, no barber has ever shaved my father. Now as I press the dead black telephone to my head, I endure a moment of terrible panic. Standing on the hospital lawn in the middle of a blinding snowstorm, I see hundreds of cousins, nephews, professional barbers, stamping their feet, just dying to shave my father. But my father wants me and me alone. It is a preference that delivers his head into my hands. Holding my father's head in my hands, my mood turns filial, surgical, tender. Touching his chin and cheeks, I seem to touch the ducts below his eyes, my eyes. Shaving my father's throat, I feel his poor pulse beat, and there is nothing that can drive me from his room and need, this repaying with a razor of a thousand, thousand favors. Except, of course, my wife.

Who will not put up with this shit, not even for a minute. Careening down the hallway, my wife turns the corner in her floral nightgown. And when she does so, she finds me staring out the window. This is the stuff our best fights are made of. I am pale, but my wife is paler. It is 4 A.M. and I still haven't put the telephone down. Advancing toward me, my wife starts our fight as she often starts our fights, with the asking of a simple question. Looking up at the ceiling, she asks me *god damn it* what time it is.

4 A.M.

What are you doing?

Answering the phone.

Is there still somebody on it?

No.

Are you going to make another call?

No.

Then why don't you put it down?

It is a good question. I look at my shoes and think about putting the telephone down.

Don't think about it, she says, just do it.

I put the telephone down and my wife asks me to look at her. I look at her and she says I said *look* at me. I look at her. My wife doesn't look good. Her eyes are bloodshot and she is $7\frac{1}{2}$ months pregnant. The print in her floral nightgown is blue and I am in the U.S. Army. Upon my shoulders, the hands of southern sergeants still hop and caw. *Lieutenant, lieutenant,* they whisper and pass the bottle to me. The bottle is filled with white lightning somebody bottled back in Alabama. Crashing with sword, cannon, rebel yell, the hillbilly radio throws us off the road, a scent of moonshine and mustard gas knocking my small car in and out of a ditch, my wife asking now about the dried blood at the edge of my hair, wanting to know, *by god,* what happened to my head.

I cut it.

How?

In a wreck.

In the car?

Yes.

Where is it?

Out there, I say and point toward the driveway. Drifting to the window, my wife gazes at the fresh dents and chips I've put in the front end of our car.

What did you hit?

I ran into a ditch.

Oh shit, she says, that's all we need.

But tonight she isn't angry, she is pale. Turning and looking down at the telephone, she asks *who was it?*

My sister.

What did she want?

For me to come home.

Why?

Because of Dad.

What about him?

He's been operated on.

Where?

His aorta, I say and tap a finger at the top of my gut, *the main trunk artery from the heart.*

My wife stares at me and I try to stare back at her. But my eyes, somehow, are out of focus. "That black abstracted look," my wife has come to call it, and I am giving it to her now, my look blackened and abstracted by moonshine and crashing cactus, a distrust that makes my wife ask if my father's operation was a *success.*

I guess.

Then why go home?

Because, I tell her, he wants me to shave him.

Shave him?

I nod and my wife rolls her eyes.

That's ludicrous, she whispers. It's maudlin and obscene.

My wife is standing under an electric light. The light is bright and there is a flower print in her nightgown. The palms of her hands are wet and her thighs are thick; our marriage is strictured, amputated, carburated, it runs on adrenalin and asthma, that profane stroke of the nose by which my wife sneezes and marks me *bastard, bastard, bastard,* you're a *bastard* if you go back and leave me stranded out here.

I look at her and she screams look at me *god damn it* I've got asthma and I'm $7\frac{1}{2}$ months pregnant. Touching her stomach, she stamps her foot: do you know that there are no locks on the doors, that I don't know a soul out here, that this house is sitting smack on top of the San Andreas Fault, that there could be an earthquake at any moment, that I can't even drive that god damned car?

Damned, dilapidated, our small car shudders and chugs atop the San Andreas Fault. Oxidized, dented, it coughs against age and neglect, the sound of its motor deflected by grime and sludge, the blue carbon of an argument into which my wife screams *Alarmist!* Your sister's an alarmist! She loves to make breathless long-distance phone calls and meet airplanes at midnight. She'll light candles and drag out snapshots. You'll drink black coffee and have intense conversations about the Republican Party and Holy Mother Church. Oh shit I can just see the two of you now!

Oh shit so can I. Back in Central Illinois where the widow lady across the street looks like Eisenhower and where a large photograph of Eisenhower stares across the kitchen at Christ above the sink. The sink will be white. It will gleam. It will be obscene and maudlin the way my sister and I drink black coffee and sort through the snapshots. The snapshots will be black and white; six black eye sockets, three opened mouths, my father, my sister and I. I will smile and touch my sister's face. I will tell her that she is beautiful; that she should get married or go to college, that she should get the hell out of this house where the cigar boxes and coffee cups are filled with tin elephants and old campaign buttons, a scent of elephant piss and stale cigar smoke filling the rooms, the rooms themselves filled with elephant hoofs and old Palm Beach suits, the campaign buttons, bamboo canes, straw hats and Atlantic City pennants of conventions long botched and elections long lost, the old ladies gathering on our front porch in the summer, muttering and crocheting black and white velveteen likenesses of Eisenhower, their spitz dogs growling and dying out back in a welter of sparkling garbage cans and white-washed elephant hoofs, my sister smiling and telling me *please* not to talk that way, me frowning and switching from black coffee to Irish whiskey, the circles under my eyes darkening toward that old drunk black blasphemy by which my father emerges at 3 A.M.

as my sister's only god. *God damn it,* my wife screams, *look at me when I talk to you!*

I look at her. My wife doesn't look good. Asthmatic, pregnant, enraged, there is something in the thickness of her fist and wrist that twists this departure toward *her* father, the 12-gauge, full-bore shock by which he packs his shotguns and deserts my wife at critical 16, leaving her forever to a fudge-making, chain smoking, waterlogged aunt, my wife and the aunt snuffling and eating fudge, a burnt scent of gut, blood, buckshot, bore-cleaner and asthma in the air, the desertion itself giving off a sense of heart attacks and ambulances, sirens and shortwave radios, the neighbors beginning to wail and gather, my wife's hale father being wheeled from a back bedroom under a burgundy blanket, the aunt screaming *deserter, deserter,* my wife standing on the front porch in one of his old coats, her pockets stuffed with shotgun shells, beef jerky, warrants for her father's arrest, her shy, cross-eyed father waving dimly from behind his thick glasses, sirens screaming, a red and yellow Rambler station wagon disappearing in the direction of Colorado, my wife just beginning to date and hyperventilate, 16½ years old, breathing in and out of a paper sack to get her breath, sitting at the kitchen table with the aunt and a boyfriend, sorting through color photographs of her father butchering an elk in Colorado, his knife flashing yellow and rose against tendon and innard, the elk itself looking shocked and maternal, a stiff hoof stuck up in the air as if to piss, my wife's shy, cross-eyed father squatting in her guts, his knife and his fists and his elbows slashing and chopping and turning this departure now into a desertion my wife can neither forget nor forgive: I won't let you go, she whispers, you can't do this to me!

Do what to you?

Desert me this way.

Like a hatchet in a closet that word falls through our upraised hands; my wife and I are fighting in miniature in the dark; the doors have been closed, locked, taped; our screams and fathers are caught in paper sacks above our heads, they balloon like captions above our fights, we hold them by the throat, our feet dangle and thrash amid shotgun shells and white-washed elephant hoofs; our marriage is a joke, a levity, a pale coil of elk gut and aorta through which we blow and trumpet our more essential hurts: *Desert* you, I whisper and ask for it, who's *deserting* you?

You're deserting me.

How?

By *leaving, leaving, leaving,* she says, every time she looks at me the phone is ringing and I'm leaving, closet doors are slamming, whiskey bottles breaking, my sister's voice a dark bell toward which I tend like a porter, redcap, doorman, this uniform reduced to its essential chintz, my commission in the U.S. Army reduced to timetables and traveling bags, a dim scrim of coin, curtsy and claim check at the end of which I await the recovery of my father, the wrath of my wife: All right, I whisper and point a finger at her, what do you want?

A husband.

You've got one.

No I don't.

I bite my lip, I make a fist, I whisper *what am I then?*

A child, she says, *a drunk,* she says, a black Catholic shadow playing against the halts and hatchets of her hyperventilation: *Help me,* she says and raises a hand on cue, *I can't breathe, I can't breathe!*

Breathless, theatrical, her symptom infers its dictum: there is nothing I can do that does not take my wife's breath away, does not refer to her father and his desertion, his red Rambler and the reddening photographs, the elk gut and the upraised butcher knife.

Against that specter I too raise a hand, promising help I know I can't provide: Don't worry, I whisper, I'll get you a paper sack to breathe in! Like slimy lightning my promise strikes below our kitchen sink, filling all our paper sacks with dark garbage, strands of hair and hairy rubber bands, torn lard cans and jagged jelly glasses. Standing now in our darkened kitchen, I imagine my wife holding a paper sack to her mouth, inhaling our garbage, her thin windpipe rattling with olive pits and greasy coffee grounds, her poor lungs a whirlwind of banana peels and fiery cornflakes. On my knees, my fingernails whitened, I rummage amid garbage sacks and drainpipes, the light below the sink sacred and hissing, my fingertips knocking against grapefruit husk and eggshell, my spine tightening toward a moment of salt, fixation, fault: God damn it, my wife screams and looks toward the kitchen, what's taking you so long in there, can't you see I'm ready to faint?

Squatting in the shadows near the kitchen sink, I whisper *no you're not,* my judgment enlarging the nostrils and oxygens of my wife's rage, defining now the marriage that we've made: We fight, I think, because it's the one thing we do well and small, I am Punch and she is Judy, whack! whack! whack! our dim fathers hold the strings; sick with our slamming doors and stubby fights, they ride above the orange grove murmuring *what did we do wrong,* the orange trees filling with tin elephants and old campaign buttons, wounded elk and elephants swaying and pissing on our lawn, white-washed elephant hoofs stomping up and down inside our garbage, our hot fists flailing inside the silk sleeves of Palm Beach suits, my wife and I enraged with our own dimensions, two dwarfs caught in an absence of paper sacks, a marriage of straw hats and bamboo canes that seem now to rise and beat against my head: muttering *God is dead,* I bang out the kitchen door to join a deeper impertinence in the living room.

I say *look* and my wife says *what?*

All of our paper sacks are filled with garbage.

Pushing past me, she disappears against a clatter of kitchen doors, drawers and garbage sacks, reappearing to whisper *fine this is just fine,* me following her the length of our house, our house a maze, a clapboard trap without a single paper sack: *you filled them all with garbage didn't you,* she whispers, tapping a finger against my chest, *now god damn you, I'm going to faint!*

No you're not.

Oh yes I am, she says, arriving before the overstuffed safeties of our living room couch: just watch me you bastard, just watch me!

Watching my wife trying to faint is a religious experience. I think of tracheotomies and mouth-to-mouth resuscitation. Against her throbbing throat I press the careful knife, pinching her nose, I clear her mouth of all old nauseas, my mouth fighting its way to her mouth through glues of elk gut and burnt gunpowder, the specific midgets of our history beginning to hoot and dance now in all our windows, my wife whispering *shit, shit, shit,* the word becoming flesh, bowing my legs and shortening my spine. Three feet tall, I back away from her. Faking it, my wife claps a hand to her forehead: oh Christ, she screams and falls onto the living room couch, I'm blacking out, I'm blacking out!

Backing out the door and down the hall, I whisper *I'll be right there.* But I can't move. Profane, predictable, my wife's fake blackout nonetheless nails me to the spot, sinks our fight in terrible intermission. Overhead, jets scream east without me. *Without me.* The thought turns me toward the bedroom. Rushing from closet to bureau to bathroom and back, I pack, stuff, cram and shut my suitcase with a bang. Through the orange grove the black exhausts of east-bound airplanes sift and filter. Against the walls and domes of international airports in Los Angeles I hear my name being called and called. Where am I? I am left behind. The thought pulls me through the living room, out the door, across the lawn. *Left behind, left behind,* it is not so much a thought as it is the sound of a door slamming, a voice booming *where the fuck do you think you're going?*

Home.

Like hell you are.

Like hell I'm not.

I turn and my wife is descending our front stairs, her feet beating white and frightened against the concrete of the sidewalk, each step she steps toward me adding to her rage: *put down that suitcase!*

Make me.

Get back in the house!

Go to hell.

Leaning her face toward me, my wife whispers *prick* and I say *bitch*. Bastard, slut, shit, whore, creep, cunt; thus we shunt and shift the issue, my father's operation drawn like smoke from the folds of our tightening fight, my foot lifting and kicking against the door of our small car.

Stop it, stop it!

Moving forward, I kick the headlight.

Idiot!

Idiotic, slow, the glass flows in a cone from my toe and my suitcase turns into a joke. When my wife touches it, my suitcase erupts. It is a strange moment. My suitcase coughs and bucks. Then a single bolt of silk seems to jump from my gut, my suitcase working like a suitcase in a circus, disgorging more than it could possibly ever hold, the air between my wife and me rupturing with brilliant color, as if many Palm Beach suits and blood-soaked flags were falling all around us, slurred snapshots and bloody hunting knives, concrete strewn with the regimental starch, stripes and silks of the 20 shirts and neckties that I've packed, enough socks, trousers and jackets to last me for weeks and months, the bright whites of my shorts and T-shirts showing bone blue against the grease spots our small car has dripped on the driveway.

Standing before me, my wife raises a hand to her mouth. It is a signal and I take it. Dropping to my knees, I begin to re-pack my suitcase. But I cannot do so fast enough. My socks and shorts are somehow too numerous, clean and neat: stacks and stacks of secret, lurid clothes I've packed behind my wife's back, enough stuff for a desertion, my wife kneeling beside me whispering *my god how long were you planning to be gone?*

Not long.

Then what were you going to do with all these clothes?

Wear them.

All of them.

No.

Then why did you pack so many?

Reaching out and grasping three white shirts and a pair of silver cufflinks, I tell my wife I wanted to have a choice and she says *choice?*

About what to wear.

Where?

To the hospital.

Whispering *oh,* my wife lifts a hand toward me. The gesture is quiet, resigned. Her hand drifts and whitens. Then she touches my face and our back door seems to slam and slam a hundred times before I understand that she has risen, turned and fled from me, something wounded and shy about the way she has moved across the lawn, as if it is *too late, too late,* now that I have packed these clothes I must carry and wear them, my wife somehow damning and commanding me to go back to Central Illinois to shave my father, a new silence gathering around our house, pinning me now to the concrete of a driveway that bucks, grunts, scoots and honks across the continent toward darkening Illinois. Turning, I follow it like a barber might follow it.

My suitcase clangs and clatters. Inside it, I carry nothing but razors, scissors, pincers, clippers; glinting brutal stuff that drives me through doors, up hospital corridors to arrive at my father's bed, my fingers flowering with blue blades and styptics, my face bending down toward my father's face, my hands getting ready somehow to shave him. I try to rise and turn from him but cannot. Narrowing my eyes, I look at my father's head. It is no longer Republican but Caesarian. White Caesarian hooks of hair curl across his temples; there is a black Caesarian depth and dignity to his nostrils, mouth and sockets of his eyes. Again, I try to rise and turn, but I feel roped and close, caught with my father in a snarl of mucous and glucose: plastic tubes hiss and curl from his nose as if he's yoked, heaving and pulling hard on a load he will never be able to pull, nuns and nurses moving in and out of his room exuding white from the white of their caps, hair, hose and teeth, to the white squeak of their shoes upon the floor. Just above my ankles, pinned to the underrigging of my father's bed, there's a plastic satchel bulging with blood and urine, the insteps of my father's feet are blue, the moons of his toenails black and lilac. Reaching out, I touch my father's hand, and the nurses pat their hair, check their watches. Answering *yes* and *no* to the complicated, incessant questions my sister asks about my father's chances (*would you say his chances are 50/50 or 9 to 1*), the nurses smile, nod and back toward the doorway, an aged Latvian priest limping up the hall at 6 A.M. with the white communion host upon which, each morning, my father coughs then chokes, *they took the catheter out last night, they put the catheter back in this morning,* the catheter moving in and out, my father asking my sister to "wrench" out his drinking glass, taking tiny sips of water and whispering *don't look at me all the time, don't look at me all the time,* frowning now and calling for a shave. It's a man's job, but stepping in front of me, my sister performs it with a smile. Leaning over his face, she pulls and stretches the skin. My father's breath is sweet, citric, overwhelming. Taking up the electric razor, my sister breathes his breath and cannot breathe herself. Averting her face, she trims his moustache: the white hairs fall on the thickened tongue, my sister picks them out with Kleenex one by one, discovering as she does a tough rim of whisker growing along the lower lip of his collapsed mouth, the blades of the razor almost rubbing gum, my sister anxious even as she shaves him to *bring him home,* stopping nuns and nurses in the hallways to whisper *I'll be so glad to get Dad home,* asking while he's still in Intensive Care if he can wear his wristwatch, glasses, own pajamas, hanging dark suits and clean shirts in his hospital closet, shining his shoes and darning his socks against the day when waking, I'll return from Southern California to help her, bundling him up and *bringing Dad home,* devising elaborate systems of bells and spoons and coffee cans by which he can call for water to drink or oil for his back, our bathtub filling with bedpans and orange enema bottles, my sister and I pampering and pampering him, my father's torso turning more leathery and batlike every day, all ribs and tendons and elbows, as if under our care and worry he were preparing somehow for flight, ready at any moment to flap, lumber and explode from his bed, banging blind against the ceiling, his bedsheets trailing, my sister and I trying with upraised hands to corner and pull him back, my father crashing through the plate-glass picture window, leaving my sister and me to drink black coffee and Irish whiskey at the Irish undertaker's office, Jimmy O'Flynn explaining that he knew our father's taste and exactly what he would have wanted, his coffin some final Palm Beach suit or bamboo cane he is going to buy, my sister sitting at O'Flynn's in black, nodding, crying and turning me with her tears back toward my house and marriage, the shy, heavy retreat my wife has beaten across our lawn, a silence against which, rising from the driveway, I stride up the steps and into the living room, heading without a word toward the telephone.

When I reach down to pick it up, my wife stands and asks me what I'm doing.

Making a phone call.

To whom?

My sister.

What for?

I've got something to tell her.

What?

That I've decided not to come home.

My wife's movement, when she makes it, is blurred and concussive. The windows shake and she stops with her face thrust up not an inch from mine whispering: oh no you don't, I'm not taking all the god damned blame.

For what?

For not letting you go.

But I don't *want* to go.

Oh yes you do, she says, I saw all those clothes. I *know* you want to go!

Then she moves her face even closer to mine, taps my chest and says now if you think I'm going to stand there on that phone and answer all your sister's bloody god damned questions about why you've decided at the last moment *not* to come home, you've got another fucking think coming!

The thought, when it comes, is slow in coming. But once it's there, it fits and fucks like a nail, spike, screw driven just above my nose between my eyes. Looking down into my wife's eyes, I can barely remember that she has fought for five full hours against my going home to shave my father, that she has ever stomped and screamed and refused to let me go home to shave my father, something machined and perfect about this hasp and hinge by which clicking, ticking and locking our fight seems to turn of its own accord, my wife and I fighting our fight now from different sides, her blue eyes holding the moment, me stepping back, assuring her that she won't have to answer any of my sister's bloody god damned questions, my wife stepping forward hissing *oh yes I will.*

No you won't. I'll tell her you're not here.

She'll call back.

We won't answer.

Oh yes we will. She'll just keep calling and calling and sooner or later we'll have to answer. Then she'll ask you to ask me if I won't please speak to her and I'll have to talk to her and do you know what she'll say? She'll start telling me about dead blood, blood clots, bloody urine and bleeding from the anus. Then she'll end by asking me to ask you at least to pray for Dad and when I don't say anything she'll offer again to pay my way if I fly home with you and I'll tell her she can't afford it, it's too expensive, but she'll say *please oh please there's a plane that gets in here at midnight* then I'll have to remind her that I've got asthma and I'm $7\frac{1}{2}$ months pregnant, but she won't buy that either so I'll finally have to tell her that I can't fly in airplanes, that I over-breathe, that I *hyper-fucking-ventilate,* that bitch sighing and thinking *what did my brother marry* well I can't take it, I refuse to go through it, just pick up that fucking god damned bag and get out of here.

It is an order that I would like to take, but cannot. Something in me wants to grab my bag, to bolt and blow through the door, but instead I lift both hands above my head and whisper look god damn it, what do you *really* want me to do?

Leave.

Why?

Because it would scare me more for you to stay.

Why?

Because of your father.

What about my father?

He's *dying*.

Dying my ass.

Every time my wife slaps me, she slaps me across the nose. And every time she slaps me across the nose, I bleed, she overbreathes. This time is no exception. With a clap and a pop, my wife reaches out and touches me. As her hand withdraws, it draws blood from both my nostrils into the sudden handkerchief I hold and press against my face. But my wife can't stop here. Even before she fits a shoulder to my chest, the living room wall crashes against my back, my wife and I sliding down the wall and our fight roaring past us like something that wants to suck us right out the door through the air terminal, out onto the runway through a hiss of air brakes and a roar of jet motors, our fight lifting us high into the sky above Southern California, our fists whistling over the Rocky Mountains and the Mighty Mississippi, the two of us stumbling and flailing right through my father's funeral into childbirth, bloody, smoking labor, middle age, old age, death, our fight refusing to conclude until we ourselves conclude, both of us huddled now with our backs pressed against the living room wall, my wife gripping my sleeve, beginning now to overbreathe, calling for a paper sack to breathe in.

Backing through the door, I back not only through the supermarket, but through the hardware store as well, dropping a stack of paper sacks on my wife's lap, backing and crab-crawling from door to door, hammering and screwdriving until I've got brass hasps and chain locks on all the doors, stuffing my clothes into my suitcase and snapping it shut, returning to squat at my wife's side, listening to the suck and flap of the paper sack as she breathes in and out, my wife turning now to look at me.

Her eyes are blue and when she rises, I rise with her. As we move through the house, our hands graze the walls. The paper sack flaps in and out, my wife locks all the chain locks I've installed, the two of us arriving before the opened front door, me picking up my suitcase and my wife dropping the paper sack from her mouth asking me to tell her *just one thing.*

What?

That I'll be able to sleep tonight.

I look at her and she claps the paper sack back over her mouth. The paper sack flaps in and out and I put my bag down whispering god damn it I thought you *wanted* me to go.

You *have* to go.

No I don't.

Yes you do. Just tell me I'll be able to sleep tonight.

The paper sack flaps in and out and I whisper you know I can't tell you you'll be able to sleep tonight.

Just say it then, you don't have to believe it.

I can't.

Yes you can.

No I can't.

Yes you can.

Beyond my wife's shoulders, orange trees wink and flicker. Under the brass and khaki of my uniform our fight begins once more to sing and gnaw, feeling like it's never going to stop, the paper sack flapping in and out, my wife snapping it from her mouth, whispering shit I'm sorry just leave, god damn it, just leave.

Again, I would like to, but I can't. Watching the paper sack flap in and out, our living room filling with sunlight, brass hasps glinting on all the doors, a stack of paper sacks strewn across the floor, I am pulled and drawn into my wife's insomnia, my face setting in its "black abstracted look," my wife whispering *oh no you don't you bastard,* grabbing me by the shoulders and shoving me out the door screaming just leave god damn it, just leave, leave, leave!

44

Punch & Judy

Even as I turn to leave, I waver and drop anchor. In the orange grove glucose carts and bottles clatter as I descend then rush back up the steps, pushing and slamming against our locked front door, my wife retreating behind her flapping paper sack, shaking her head and fist as she backs into the shadows at the far end of the living room, rounding the corner and disappearing with a woosh and slam of the bedroom door, me turning now toward Central Illinois, leaving for the first, thousandth and final time to shave oh shave my fallen father.

Strong Is Your Hold O Love

SHE screamed what did he think she did all day without food to feed them and soap to do the wash with, but you don't care do you? And he said yes I do, I told you I got something going today, I'll go get it right now. Then as he opened the door she asked him if he'd picked up her books at the library and he closed the door shaking his head, but remembered the Tide as he reached down for the ready handle of the Home Laundry Size, thought how often and how wrong he was and returned with the weight of that box in one hand and the groceries in the other, hoping that she would still be up so that he could put each down in front of her and promise that it would go differently from now on. But she was in bed.

Now the tips of her toes against his ankle, the hair of her head against his shoulder, and he touches her wrist and she does not move. He takes it in his hand, feels her pulse against his palm, looks at her face and what he has done to her with his choppy impatience, his hysteria to assault a new day every day and wring something new out of it, banging out the door and into the car, his insides boiling with possibility, leaving her stranded at the door almost every morning in tears.

It is almost 1 A.M. now and he is heartily sorry that he is alone, that he has shoved her off into an uneasy sleep with the sound of the squabble still in their room; and this morning the battle when she insisted that he take time to write down what had to be remembered at the Safeway, he rose above her when she snapped at him, cocking his fist with a filthy and nasal showing of teeth, crouched and drew back his fist looking at her forehead. He bit his lip, faked the blow, she cowered sobbing, then he said into the back of her neck as he held her hands down on the bed that he was sorry and he promised he'd never hit her.

There is a strand of hair fallen across her forehead in an arc over her eyebrow. Moving toward her, taking his chances, he picks it up, grinds the hairs between his thumb and index finger, then drops them above her ear and falls back into his pillow, that clarity still rough on his fingertips.

His wife asleep in the fine wreck the kids have made of their room. It is difficult for him to believe that she is here with him now, has partaken of and overseen the collision and free play that have made their room as right and as much theirs as it ever could be; that from the bad beginnings she has stuck with him to this and now holds as much of it and as tightly as he does; that she must have her moments like this too, when it was all as inevitable and right as the pink and upturned sink of the Child-Size Kitchen in the corner. He lifts his head off the pillow and glories in the screaming yellow door that almost opens into the dresser on which a stack of folded diapers is toppled against a bottle of Aquamarine lotion and a broken bookend. With his foot still under the blanket he pushes against the huge blue toybox that's jammed against the bottom of the bed, and it barely moves because, he remembers, it's hooked on a fray in the rug. Hanging and balanced on its edges are Clarabelle Cow, Raggedy Ann, the Farmer in the Dell (turn the crank and see the farmers act out each story), a pounding board, Porky Pig and a plaid frilled doll buggy over which his own trousers are draped. He settles back with a perfect sense of relaxation and rightness and wishes all three of them would come bursting in the door right now and throw themselves on him and rub their foreheads, cheeks and noses into his as he tickled them on their springy and explosive ribs.

He rolls toward her and thinks perhaps he ought to share this moment with her while it lasts. Because after the alarm if she touched him or they fell in with him and crawled over him, he would rise sharply with what he had to get done that day, put them down on two feet on the rug, yell at her above the buzz of his razor that he had to get going, let's go with the breakfast.

He bends down toward her so that his head rests beside her smoothly clothed shoulder, so that the profile of her mouth is thrown above him against the wall, so that the purity of her face is hollowed and bound by the darkness of her eyes and hair — their room as cool and cluttered as those first nights in motels when she had slept beside him after he had murdered one by one the phantoms of his long wait, and the sheets of their bed seemed to stretch out over traveling bags and in-laws and all the busy troubles that awaited them when they returned and owned up — as cool as that porcelain quietude after he had shot it all and tried to piss away that final tenderness, as if he could widen himself with one of her bobby pins and splatter cool and final blood on the barbed and unperfumed world that waited for him when he was through with her and ready to return to it and fight.

He should awaken her and tell her how much better it is now that they are five and at wide-open war with the bastard world that surrounds them.

He lifts her pajama tops, slides his wide-open hand onto her ribcage and pauses when he feels the smallness of her breathing, as if he held all of her in the width of his hand. Or he knows that he should not commit every wrong familiarity that their room and bed would allow just so he doesn't wake the kids. He should awaken her with gentleness and vows, yet at the moment that he knows that most certainly, he moves his hand from her ribs to her breast, softened by sleep, obscured by her position, and she turns sharply from him and says something like no, and clutches the blanket to her throat. He is left there with his hand on her side, his forearm the distance between them, knowing with a near smile that she wouldn't let him go that far. Yet he is shocked by the sound she made, like a cry from a little girl.

He looks at the wall through a halo of frazzled hair that stands around her ear, kisses the back of her neck, and when she shrugs, moves his hand down her waist and rests three fingers there. And because he is wrong and pausing he puts his index finger on her ribs, his small finger on her hip, his thumb on her spine, and hunches up against her. In a way he could stop here, except that he wonders how violent her resistance would be and if at the end of it he would still feel this way and could tell her about it. Or perhaps he should wait until the alarm slams at them and then offer a few answers over breakfast and a kindness at the door. He moves his hand over the uterine slack of her stomach and begins to knead it. She screams stop it and rolls away from him still holding the blanket in her fist. He buzzes in the chest and face and for a moment could grab her, turn her over, force his face into hers, then roll over to his own side of the bed and forget her, wake up and murder the morning.

But he stays in that warm and wakeful middle ground and begins again with care. He hunches his shoulder down on the mattress, pulls her pajamas away from her back and begins to stroke her spine with a new and cunning control, using only the back of his nails, so slowly and lightly that he burrows down into the certainty of his method, lifts her pajamas higher and knows he can't go wrong. He breathes and murmurs, strokes and restrokes the length and width of her back with a sensitivity and thoroughness over her kidneys and shoulderblades that astounds him.

When she shudders finally and relaxes, admitting the scale and the harmlessness of his effort, he puts a leg between hers, his lips against her back and mutters over and over again just relax, until the fragrance of her skin and her stillness make him move. With his left hand he pulls her pajama pants away from her lower back and begins to stroke softly further and further down. Finally she stiffens and begins to shake her head into the pillow. He moves up on his elbow and says, I'm just trying to get you to relax. She says don't, and he says just relax and begins again. She reaches back, pushes his hand away. I love you, he says and begins to stroke her back again. Just try to relax.

Watching her tight profile on the pillow, he moves his hand back and forth, working slowly, wishing she weren't asleep and he didn't have to awaken her to her anger, will and the dazzling brawl that's bound to happen. Yet he can barely keep from reaching around her to her breasts and getting the thing going with a bang. Or as his hand moves slowly he wishes she were dreaming and he could move miraculously onto her and into her, without having to rouse, strip or spread her. She'd open her eyes to the movement of her own body and he'd tell her what a fine wreck their room was and how lucky they were to be there and if she didn't understand, he'd explain until they both fell asleep knowing.

When he reaches her pajama pants again, he moves his hand over her buttocks, between her legs, and begins to push her pajama pants into her with the middle finger of his right hand. She rolls and sits up facing him screaming you bastard and swings at him. He grabs her wrist, forces her back down on the pillow and says I want to talk to you and love you. She digs the nails of her free hand into his side, which with the flexing and the leverage he can stand and almost enjoys, and her head falls back in blank exasperation. I love you, he says into her neck, and she says I'm going to scream if you don't get off, oh god I'm sick. But he doesn't move and she begins to scream louder and more brutally than he ever imagined anyone could, as if she were going to blow his insides and the walls out and kill all the dangerous waiting bastard neighbors with her wail. He begins to shake her shoulders yelling stop it, then she starts sobbing and gagging, which he knows occurred to her when she heard her own scream, but still is stark and unnerving in the corner of their bed.

Holding her shoulders he says I'm sorry I didn't know you were that far asleep I just needed you I'm sorry and she begins to say over and over you hate me don't you, looking him in the eyes while he shakes his head, finally feeling the pressure under his nails, and releases her arms. No I love you, he says, and looks at her forehead, his answer as wrong as his eyes. He moves his face over her shoulder, puts his arms around her, tries not to lean on her as he looks at the wall. He wishes now not so much for a miraculous oneness, but that the house wasn't so cold and her hair wasn't pulled back and held by a rubber band, so that at least he could put his hands in there. Kneeling up, lifting his arms from her shoulders, he says I love you into her temple. She pushes him away, picks up her pillow and says, I'm sleeping in the living room and you'd better not follow me.

As she squeezes out between the dresser and the door he says, do you love me? When he hears her flop on the broken sofa in the living room, he follows her, kneels in the cold above her turned-away face, puts both hands beside her and says again, do you love me? She doesn't answer. She lies curled in the mean, glancing light from the streetlight, over a hairy rip in the sofa. He wants to pick her up in the blanket, squeeze back through the door lifting her high over the dresser, feeling his chest flex with all of her there against his face, put her to bed and hear her say yes she did, and sleep in watchful contrition where she lies now. He says, Pat, and she says nothing. He says, I'm going to carry you back into bed and sleep out here myself. He pushes his hands under her shoulders and knees. Don't touch me she says. Standing above her he says, aren't you cold? No. Let me carry you back in. Shutup. Do you love me? I hate you. He stands there for a moment. Then I'll at least get you another blanket.

As he digs through the dark sharpness of the toybox for the quilt, he knows that if it were him he'd at least say yes he loved her just to put her to rest no matter how tired he had been, but she is small and obstinate in some ways.

Yet as he walks to her with the quilt he feels he could stay up all night waiting on her, and if he reached out into the cold right now, he could lock hands and shoulders and struggle with that new confidence, grapple with it and glory in it all night long.

He spreads the quilt over her carefully, picks up her feet, tucks them in, then fits it over her shoulders, under her chin, and she takes it in her fist and shudders down into it. He smiles at her when she accepts it that way, puts his mouth to her ear and says now do you love me? She snuggles deeper into the quilt and doesn't answer. He asks her again. Wrinkling up her nose, she says leave me alone. He stands there. Just say you love me. She doesn't answer. I got the quilt for you now just say you love me. She starts rocking her head back and forth on the pillow and moaning softly. It hurts him to see her do that and he thinks she doesn't know what she's doing to me by doing that, the way I feel about her right now. He puts his hand under his T-shirt and says just say you love me and we'll both be able to go to sleep. Oh god she says. Say it. She rolls toward him with her eyes wide open. You selfish bastard if you don't leave me alone I'm going to start screaming again. Selfish did you say, he says, and screams, go ahead, slamming his hands down on the arm of the sofa, straining on her smallness, lifting one end of it chest high and dropping it crashing to the floor. She rolls off, runs into the kitchen, and he hears one of the kids start in upstairs. I'm sorry he screams behind her and she slaps both hands into the sink and begins sobbing between her arms.

When he touches her shoulder she collapses onto the cold floor, which he thinks is a favorite trick of hers — but this time he is glad she has done it. He lifts her limp and complete form off the floor and she murmurs god oh god, again and again. He lifts her over the dresser, puts her down on the bed, covers her and drives quietly up the stairs three at a time in his bare feet to their year-old son, who is standing up, yelling and shaking the side of his crib.

Michael boy he says swinging him up, cradling his hefty weight in his right arm, moving across the floor toward the window with kindness and control, jiggling him softly, saying Michael boy, Michael boy, until his son stops crying and puts his temple against his cheekbone. He breathes deeply with Michael there high on his chest heaving and quieting down, his right arm ready to hold him all night long in the name of love and confidence and her below sobbing. He puts his hand behind Michael's head and pauses so that her gasps come at the top of his every breath. He rocks his son back and forth, wants to go to her, but can feel himself hanging there at the door, his T-shirt across his shoulders and the brutal enthusiasm with which he woke her like a hatchet in his hand.

He rocks Michael back and forth and begins to murmur all the things his son might like to hear about eagles, antelopes, buffalo, wigwams, warpaths and the Winnebago, until he realizes that he is asleep and the house is quiet. He puts Michael in the crib, pats his back with a left hand that works like a tender trip-hammer and climbs back down the stairs quietly two at a time, wishing there were something he could still do for her.

He squeezes softly between the door and the dresser and looks at her in their bed. The cold mess around her. Dolls and winter coats, receiving blankets and rubber pants, dirty towels, red boots, ripped corduroys and thin plastic belts with huge rusted buckles stuffed in corners, stacked around the bed and toybox, spilling out of the closet and dresser drawers, as if the floor should be

puddled and ribboned with ice and cold weeds should be growing in clumps along the wall and she should wake to search
through thorns for clothes enough to put on the girls and Michael
in the screaming morning, in the chill hell of desertion and desti-
tution in which he has left her from the beginning. He kicks the
cool *Golden Book of Child's Verses* from below his right foot
and as the furnace goes on, feels the unvented dryer in the basement like a time bomb in his stomach. Her father had said that
accumulation of lint would go like TNT and the copper tubing
to it was so dangerous Sears wouldn't install it anymore and
crimped on top of it, but he had no time for that, not a minute
god damn it, he had to get going and with it, to strangle on his
own brutal and private hope like a blowtorch caught in his craw
every morning, and if he returned one night to ashes and ice,
that was her tough luck.

He picks up the *Golden Book* and puts it in the toybox. He
hangs his trousers on the closet door, puts the baby buggy in the
corner, hangs the hoods of the girls' coats atop his trousers and
puts three dolls in the box. He gathers up the dirty towels, wash-
cloths, undershirts, underpants, training pants, corduroys, sweat-
ers and leotards and throws them down to the bottom of the
basement stairs. As he squeezes back through the door he decides
that he can move the toybox into the hall closet without waking
her. She has been after him to do it, and if it fits, if he doesn't
have to force it or jam it or empty it and tip it on its side, there
will be no problem.

He takes the broken bookend and the Aquamarine lotion off
the dresser, puts them on the girls' sink, then on the floor. He
pushes on the dresser until the rug curls up under it and stops
him. He looks at her, kneels and lifts the dresser first at one end,
then the other, pulling at the rug and straightening it. He stuffs
the clothes into the drawers, closes them, and hugging the dresser
from the front, lifts it inch by inch until it is free of the door and

rests directly in front of the hot-air register. He puts a popcorn pushtoy, four wooden milk bottles and a plastic baked potato in the toybox and looks at the girls' kitchen. To get the door fully opened he will have to stack the sink and stove on the refrigerator — if he doesn't want to surround her bed with them. He jams the sink against the ceiling, pats the stove, which is off center and unsteady in the middle of the stack, then scoops up a pile of sheets and unironed shirts and blouses and stuffs them in the wicker basket on the floor of the closet, his trousers and the coats on top of that, and closes the door.

The toybox is heavy. He puts it down, slips into clean, shrunken underpants and a pair of cut-off sweatpants he takes from the doll-size porta-crib, which he folds up and props against the wall out of his way. Trembling over the length of the toybox, he lifts it free from the snag in the rug, tries to push it, but the rug stops him. Twice he measures the width of the box, walks to the door without looking at or moving his hands, but it's too late, quiet and uncluttered to accept that quarter inch and the faint hook of how he got it in here in the first place — too still to extract Clarabelle Cow, the blue lawnmower, telephone and baby grand piano from the tangled depths of the toybox and strew them and the rest of it in sharp plastic piles around her bed, admitting the magnitude, complexity and danger of the job he is trying to do quickly and simply.

So he grunts, humps, lifts the toybox into the door and wedges it there, screeches into his teeth when the blue wood cuts into and settles against the yellow doorjamb and the toys shift loudly. He lifts his right foot and the long bony toes of it, and kicks the mother-fucking whore son of a bitch with the ball of his foot and jams it a little tighter. He turns and she is sitting up with her eyes closed, her fists in front of her face, and she begins to say oh god no, over and over.

He says I couldn't sleep and she says you're insane. He slams his palm down on the edge of the toybox and screams what the shit do you mean I was trying to move this for you, but she says oh god you're insane. He puts his shoulder to the toybox, jams it another inch, falls on his knees, beats the floor with the heels of his fists and she starts screaming. He crawls out of the room over the toybox, hesitates when he hears Michael upstairs, bursts out the back door, jumps a fence and begins barefoot and furiously to run a path that cuts through a cemetery, past a horse barn, three cattle barns, the 13th hole, a row of 15 asphalt tennis courts, and ends in a concrete walk that leads through the only opened gate of a football stadium in which there are 94 rows of seats rising 160 feet all around, each row one perfect stride atop the other.

He sprints the first 40 yards of the alley with teeth bared as if he were driving up the side of that stadium, his feet and the frozen ground slammed out of his consciousness by the chop of the single breath he holds and the wedge of the toybox against which he drives knees and fists. When he eases up, sucks for breath, looks at and feels his white feet on the frozen ground, he moves up a bit on his toes, protecting the veins he feels vaguely in his arches, and decides he's going to run the stadium stairs, even if they bleed him to pneumonia and blank-ass death.

The cemetery is a furious, intestine and dead world of broken statuary, tombstones and icy pines, and he runs it and searches it as if his rage might make a difference. As if he might leave some wrecked change in his path. He slows, seizes a small tombstone below a single thin pine, puts his shoulder to it, digs his fingers into its inscription and strains, feeling her curled in its guts, with fists and screams, dead to his slow push. He heaves, feeling the threat of a tear, the threat of a long recovery among the bastards of this mother-fucking world son of a bitch, falls on his elbows, breathes heavily, pushes up on one knee, stares at the ragged edge of his sweatpants and wonders if Michael is letting her sleep or if he is still screaming for her or him.

He springs up, sprints the long last hill toward the stadium, runs past the horse barn, cattle barns, golf course and tennis courts until he is out of breath, slows, lets his arms fall to his sides, his head fall back, and can see her climbing those dark stairs toward screaming Michael.

He sets his eyes on the entrance to the stadium, settles to a steady pace and imagines that he climbs each stair behind her, looking into the small of her back, braced and climbing in pure and determined concern, in kind anticipation, distant enough to make no mistake or interference, yet close enough to see and feel the clotty necessity, the confused pain with which she must climb no matter how tricky or impossible her job has become.

As she moves up each stair he can barely keep his hands from her shoulders, can barely keep from stopping her there and telling her I'm back I'll take you to bed and fix Michael a bottle now don't worry I'm sorry I love you.

But she climbs. He watches her hand grip the top of the rail, her knuckles rise with the strain as she takes the last step and pushes through the door. As she lifts Michael out of the crib, he runs into the stadium through Gate 22, starts down the long rows of seats telling her he'll run right downstairs and get Michael a bottle, you just hold him a second I'll be right back — imagining that he bounds down those dark piddling stairs, fixes a bottle in a hurry and swings back up there with it, quiets him quickly and takes her back to bed where she belongs, but he gets going too fast toward the bottom, falling except that he keeps his feet hitting every other row, jumps the rail onto the track to stop himself and scrapes his right elbow and knee on the cinders.

Kneeling there with the heel of his hand against his cheek, touching the dirty scrape along his forearm, he sees Michael swing around to look for his bottle, sees her arm slip with his sudden movement. He stands up, brushes the dirt off his knee and says don't try it with him in your arms I'm telling you, but she leans over, a strand of hair falls across her eye, she picks up the empty plastic bottle, walks to the top of the stairs, strains around Michael's shoulder to judge her first step. No you don't he screams and bounds over the rail, starts up, I'll be up there in a minute just put him back down and let him cry if he wants to I'm coming. She frowns and with a fragile flip of her wrist, and bend of her knees, throws the bottle out and he almost stumbles between rows 44 and 45 imagining that he barely catches it as it hits the hard kitchen floor, pops high into the air and flips once on the nipple. I'll just take this and fill it he screams, with fists pumping, you just stay there where you are don't make another move I'll be up there with this in a second. She hesitates tightly and quietly at the top of the stairs as if she were deciding which foot to step down with first, or perhaps, he prays as he moves over row 64, she's decided to put him back in the crib and wait for me after all because I'm on my way just wait one minute. She reaches out tentatively with her right foot, stops, brings it back, touches the wall with her left hand, tucks her chin over Michael's shoulder, strains forward to look down, and as he moves over row 84, he sees the toes of her right foot settle on the edge of the first step, Michael swing around and away from her to look for his bottle, he screams watch it, her eyes tighten, her hand misses the rail, and he screams I've got you as they fall, and his hands hit the top of the stadium, his feet leave row 94, he is terribly over them awakening them with kisses, and grabs the neck of a darkened floodlight, swings into a brick wall, holds himself there praying that they will move.

Murphy Agonistes

PROUD, the sons of Mississippi

hack up

the national nerve, burn it
hide it in a shallow grave, the
flashbulbs of the FBI explode
almost four years ago and

Murphy has to laugh: I never thought I'd be getting married
in Mississippi, he says, it's ominous, unreal.

Pregnant, pale, his 19-year-old bride rides beside him in his
carbon-belching Chevrolet.

Do you realize, Murphy says, how many murderers have gone
untried in this state? I'll bet there are thousands of them walking
free out there right now, *the bigoted sons of bitches!*

Breaking across the broken pines of Northern Mississippi

Murph's voice cracks at 19
against the bedsheets of the
Ku Klux Klan and

I can almost see them out there right now, he says, their horses,
crosses, torches.

Asthmatic, delicate, his wife's profile nods and sniffs.

For almost a century now, Murphy says, Mississippi has been
a blight on the national conscience, the Ku Klux Klan a cancer

against which his wife sneezes

and

Murphy looks at her: you're listening to me aren't you?

Yes.

It frightens you doesn't it?

Yes.

Then why are you acting so distracted?

Because, she says, there's something that frightens me more.

What?

this

You love me don't you, she says, you're not marrying me just because I'm pregnant?

Almost four years later, that question flames and flares in Murphy's gut. Having received his first fair share of the sodium pentothal of this world, Murphy lies in a criblike bed in one of the postoperative rooms of a large Veterans Hospital, moves his hands over the sheets below him

while the crows of Mississippi

hop and caw in the roses and

sutures of an appendectomy

that leaves Murphy dreaming of needles, the white bedsheets of the Ku Klux Klan. Opening his eyes, Murphy thinks of needles, is certain they have jammed the sodium pentothal through his eyelids into his eyes, so deep into his brain he'll never be able to see, sleep or wake again, then Murphy is vomiting into a curved dish pressed below his chin.

The dish is held by a strong blond hand. Looking at it, Murphy feels both guilt and outrage. For a moment he is certain that he has gotten drunk, uncontrollably and inexcusably drunk, the loose, dribbling shock of the vomit scorching like whiskey drunk then vomited back up again, a voice whispering *there, there,* Mr. Murphy, everything is going to be all right. In answer, Murphy shakes his head, moans, pushes the dish away. As he sits there deciding whether or not to wipe the back of his hand across his mouth, Murphy remembers how, with the hospital smock pushed up around his chest, a kindly, middle-aged lady doctor shoved her finger up his ass and asked him where it hurt, hers the first in an interminable number of fingers shoved up his ass, everybody in the hospital, it seemed, shoving a finger up his ass, orderlies, janitors, hospital policemen, Murphy closing his eyes, breathing deep, trying not to vomit again.

Behind his eyes there is a dark and coagulated stupidity. Opening them, he looks down at his gut. His groin is shaven, blood-flecked, gray. To the right of his navel there is a six-inch stitch of piano wire. With the tip of his finger, Murphy touches it. When he feels nothing, he wants to lie back down and the nurse whispers *why don't you lie back down now Mr. Murphy?* Shaking his head, Murphy tries to lower himself toward the bed. But the nurse catches him before he can even get an elbow into the mattress. Taking his head in her right hand and bracing his back with her left, she says *there, there, Mr. Murphy, you shouldn't be trying to do anything so strenuous so soon.*

Too soon, too soon, Murphy's sleep returns him to Mississippi. Where it's incessantly Saturday afternoon in September and Murphy's getting married almost four years ago on broken linoleum in an office off the main street of Hernando. Outside, the crows hop from pine tree to pine tree. Inside, the justice of the peace asks for trouble: Michael Murphy, he says, do you take this sweet girl to be your lawful wedded wife?

"I do" undoes so much.

Married, white, 19, Murphy drives his smoking Chevrolet deeper into Mississippi: don't cry, he tells his wife, I love you. Everything will be all right.

But what if it won't be all right? What if we've made a terrible mistake?

Against the blotted logic of her handkerchief, pale Murphy proposes Mexico: that's what we'll do, he says, we'll keep on driving. We'll go all the way to Mexico. I'll be a carpenter and you'll have your baby.

But what if you can't get a job?

I'll get a job.

But what if you can't?

I will.

Where?

In Mexico City or maybe Acapulco.

I'm so worried.

About what?

About us.

What about us?

Just *us* that's all.

That night, exhausted and breathing through their mouths, they lie in a Jim Crow motel with the white sheets pulled up under their chins. Through the patterns in the wallpaper, the acrylic crows of Mississippi hop and caw, Murphy's voice catches in a fretwork of fear and care: we can't go back to Illinois, he says, I refuse to lose you to your pregnancy. People will berate and worry us. We'll have to marry in The Church. I won't let that happen. I love you too much. We can't go back to Illinois.

But they return, return. And Murphy's Mississippi takes him as it must through a six-month hitch in the army, $3\frac{1}{2}$ years of college, part-time job after part-time job, Murphy's marriage returning him again and again to the night of his appendectomy.

Which begins with the progressive flattening of the right rear tire of his carbon-belching 1957 Chevrolet, which, parked on a steep, dead-end hill in front of his house, will be impossible to jack up if the tire finally flattens and he has to replace it with the spare. Wondering from time to time if you can fill a car tire with a football pump, Murphy realizes that if he is ever going to get his car off the hill he is going to have to somehow find the ignition key, which, dead drunk, he lost on the church lawn three nights before, his wife reminding him again and again that he has *to find the key to the car,* tomorrow's my day to drive the kids to preschool, she says, *I've got to have that key.* She is bent over the sink, doing the dishes. She is wearing one green rubber glove, one yellow rubber glove. There is steam in her face and as Murphy watches her he can see himself on his hands and knees in front of the stone angels of St. Matthew's Church, looking for his car key. He knows he will never find it. And he knows his wife knows he will never find it. He will make a game of it. Hand in hand he will lead his son, Michael, down the alley to the church, promising to buy him an ice-cream bar if he finds the car key. But it won't end that simply. In about three days, when the right rear tire of his battered, carbon-belching 1957 Chevrolet is completely flat, a panel truck with crossed keys painted on its doors will show up. And it will cost Murphy anywhere from $8 to $10 to get the door opened and another key made for his car, his wife turning toward him now, her green and yellow gloves dripping water on the floor, wanting to know *god damn it* if he's been listening to her.

Yes.

Then what are you going to do about *the key?*

Find it.

When?

Now.

Oh no you're not.

Murphy looks at her and she says *now* you're going to the store.

What for?

Because, she says, three nights ago you got dead drunk and invited a bunch of people over here tonight, insisted that they come, *wouldn't take no for a god damned answer,* his wife bending forward and scrubbing at the dishes, trying, Murphy knows, to surprise him with this reminder about a party which, three nights ago, he'd insisted and insisted upon giving, trying to hit him with it, to punish him with the cash she'll make him spend on chips, dips, cheeses, pumpernickels, giving him a list and insisting he buy everything on it, that and the money he'll have to give to the locksmith grinding in his guts, his 4-year-old son rushing into the kitchen now, Murphy snapping him up and lifting him high over his head, tickling him on the ribs, spinning with him in a giggling circle.

Put him down.

In a minute.

Put him down!

Go to hell.

Like a hot towel, the raw contralto of his wife's scream seems to lash around his head, to strangle and astound him as he spins. Then his son, whom Murphy is slowly lowering to the floor, reaches out and nips him on the stomach. Murphy lets out a howl. He bit me, Murphy screams, you made Michael bite me on the stomach!

Staggering and clutching at his gut, Murphy hits the kitchen table with his fist, makes the proclamation he's been wanting to make all afternoon long: I've changed my mind, he screams, there isn't going to be a party in this house tonight! If any of your sniveling friends come creeping up to my door, I'll knock them down, I'll stomp all over their wives, they'll wish they'd never heard the name of Murphy!

Stunned, succinct, his wife whirls and shakes her green-gloved fist in his face: you're insane, she screams, you're out of your mind if you think I'm going to disappoint our friends or let you slop up all this beer you're crazy!

She throws open the refrigerator door, Murphy slams it, tells her to take all that beer and cram it: I demand and deserve a little privacy, he screams, and I'm going to get it by god if I have to get it over your dead body

> hanging in his closet, the
> dumb glow-coat of Murphy's
> privacy staining the floor

then he is out the door, leaping off the front porch, landing with a thud on a sidewalk that calms him as he follows it to the back of his house, the far side of his tilted, ramshackle garage.

Urinating, Murphy knows he hasn't meant a word of what he's said just now. It's all a fake, all a show. Overhead, the new moon moves in the evening sky. Shutting his eyes, Murphy tries to rid himself of his afternoon. Not just the fight, but all of it. Then he hears Michael playing on the front sidewalk with his shovel and he knows he has to return and make amends. Rounding the corner, he bends and gives his son a hug. You wait right here Michael boy, he says, Dad will be right back out.

When Murphy opens the front door, his wife is standing at the far end of the hallway, looking at him. Moving through the living room to the dining room, Murphy takes, from a miniature wicker basket atop the mantel, his money and shopping list for the store.

As he turns to leave, his wife says wait a minute, what are you doing?

Going to the store.

What for?

We can't have all these people coming over here tonight with nothing for them to eat.

Following him across the living room, his wife hisses: what

people? After what you've done do you think I'm going to let anyone in that door?

Stepping in front of Murphy, she says: now call them. Get on the phone and tell every last one of them that tonight is off!

Stuffing his money and grocery list into his pants pocket, Murphy says, we can't call them now, it's almost 7 o'clock.

Reaching out, Murphy puts his hand on the doorknob and his wife whispers: all right by god, if you won't call them, I will!

Her hands still gloved in green and yellow rubber gloves, his wife picks up the phone whispering, I'll call them, I'll call them *all!* Biting her lower lip, she fumbles and dials a number, then as if she hasn't done it, she slams the phone back down, lifts a fist to her mouth and talking into a yellow glove as if it were a phone, she whispers, hello? The party's off, that's right, the party's off. My husband has decided he'd rather scream at me than get drunk tonight. Would you please call everybody and tell them that *I'm going to kill myself?*

Before she can pick the phone up and slam it back down again, Murphy's in front of her, telling her to take it easy. For an instant she seems to be listening to him. But then she whirls, is halfway up the stairs, stopping, swaying, screaming go on! Go to the store! When you get back I'll be dead!

He waits until he hears a door slam, then he climbs to her. Sobbing, she's stretched face down on the bed, both gloved fists wound into the bedspread. Sitting down beside her, Murphy says, I'm sorry I lost my temper, but when you screamed at me, I couldn't help it.

Then he puts his hand on her back and says, now you just stay where you are until you feel like getting up. When I get back, I'll finish the dishes and give Michael his bath.

As quietly as he can, Murphy gets up from the bed, walks to the door. As he pushes it open, his wife raises her head from the pillow and says, go ahead, go to the store. But if I've got any guts, when you get back, I'll be dead.

Dim, deadly, a thousand plastic Christs deify the dashboards of dented Plymouths and Fords throbbing and idling in the supermarket parking lot. Stunned by sunset and cigar smoke, they outstretch their arms to a world of semen, rayon, celery stalks. Casting his afternoon in such plastic as Christs are made of Murphy

> sees himself squatting on the
> floor of the bedroom closet. Candles
> gutter, prayers shudder up the sleeves
> of overcoats and

Michael says Daddy, where are we going?

To the store.

What for?

To get you an ice-cream bar and to give your mother a chance to calm down

> to detect the scent of stamped
> semen on the closet floor and

as he steps onto the checkerboard floor of the supermarket, the dim admissions of Murphy's afternoon are lost in the MUZAK that wobbles in the yellow walls, the carts that clash against the doors, the dense ligaments that creak in the knees of haggard housewives kneeling to select their wares. Haggard, irredeemable, the housewives squat and scurry along the aisles of the supermarket, their King Korn Redemption Stamps clutched in their fists, their headaches defined by Crisco, Klear Wax, cottage cheese — the scratched indices of grocery lists off which they tick another week of felicity and

> grease, Murphy thinks, is
> thicker than semen.

Striding past mop handles, rolling pins and detergents, he sees in the open countenance of Mr. Clean the closed joke of his bed-room closet. Measured against pork chops and iron-on patches, Drano and birthday candles, Murphy's afternoon is laughable; a grease spot on the closet floor. Finding neither herself nor her husband in the frilly lace rayon panties Murphy has stuffed so carefully into the toe of an overshoe, his wife will rise from the bed, walk past the closet, down the stairs

and into a party, Murphy thinks,

which will whirl in about an hour

around my head.

And it does.

Undone now at 2 A.M. by an atmosphere of flat beer and stale cigarette smoke, Murphy and his wife get slowly back to the game of having been left alone together again. Interrupted by the party Murphy denied then forced upon her, it is his wife's turn now. Murphy knows it and waits. His wife knows it and sits in a chair across from him. But because she expects him to, he cannot look at her. He takes off his shoes, and deciding to alter the game, makes the first move. Well, he says, and rises from his chair, I guess I'd better get this place cleaned up, hadn't I?

Why?

Pretending not to hear her question, Murphy begins to gather up ashtrays, beer cans, purple apple cores, dishes of glazed, greasy cheese. When he tries to pick up the half can of beer that's sitting in front of his wife, she says, as he knew she would, that's mine, leave it where it is.

Afraid just yet to obey her too quickly, Murphy picks up the beer and pours it into her half-empty glass. As the foam hovers, then spills over the rim, he tries again to anticipate her.

He says, I'm sorry I wasn't in a very talkative mood tonight, but I had a good time.

She watches him pick up three beer cans and an ashtray before she answers him. No you didn't have a good time, she says. That's why you invited these people over isn't it? To prove you couldn't have a good time?

Certain he was about to admit that to himself, Murphy cannot stand to hear his wife say it, cannot resist the impulse to grumble, answer back. Setting the beer cans down, he shakes his head and says slowly, we had them over because we *both* wanted to.

When he bears down on it, Murphy's lie betrays him. He is so unsure of what he is going to say next, he looks directly into his wife's eyes. Catching him there, she says, why did you act the way you did? Why didn't you talk to anybody? Why did you sit there and sulk all night long?

As calmly as he can, he says, *I didn't sulk all night long,* yet even as he repeats and denies it, his wife's question so dares the brawl he thought he was trying to avoid, Murphy doesn't know whether to thank her or hit her.

Looking straight up into his eyes, she says, oh yes you did, you sat there in that god damned chair in the corner and *sulked all night long.*

Sitting back down, Murphy looks at her and she says, you can't do this to me you know.

Do what to you?

Ignore me this way.

I'm not ignoring you.

Oh yes you are.

No I'm not.

Yes you are.

Standing up, she points a finger at Murphy's nose. Do you know, she says, when the last time you made love to me was?

No.

Guess.

About a week ago.

Ha!

How long then?

3½ weeks! 3½ full god damned weeks since you've laid a hand on me!

Adroit and flat-handed, she reaches down and slaps Murphy across the mouth. I'm sick of you, she says, you don't love me, you don't love Michael, you don't love anything except your *precious god damned privacy!* Then she lunges at the door whispering now I'm going out to get *laid,* to get *fucked, screwed, raped* by the first guy who comes along!

When the door slams, Murphy rises and begins immediately to pay the quick piaculative pence of beer can, ashtray, cheese plate; after cleaning the house from stem to stern, he clatters up the stairs and steals once more into the cluttered confines of his bedroom closet.

At precisely 3:30 A.M., the withered root of Murphy's appendix catches fire. Rising from the sheets in pain, he straightens out from heel to hip, pushes the framework of the bed, claws at the pillow slip, and rolling away from her, tries not to wake his wife. But when his bare feet slap the floor, she turns and says: what's the matter with you, what the hell are you doing?

The pain in his side scrapes and sparks, then flames again. Above its roar Murphy whispers: there's a terrible pain in my side, I'd better get to the hospital and have it checked.

His wife screws her face into the pillow and whispers: no, no.

This is too much. I can't take it, I can't believe it, this is the end.

Dressed, maudlin, bent double with a blowtorch in his side, Murphy descends the stairs, picks up the phone, calls a cab, shuffles into Michael's room, kisses his son on the forehead, pats him on the shoulder and turns to confront his wife in the hallway: go back to bed, he says, I'll phone and let you know what they decide.

Who decides?

The doctors.

Where are you going?

To the Veterans Hospital.

You're not a veteran.

You don't have to be, they'll take you if you've just been in the service.

Liar.

She follows him down the hall and turns on the light.

Where are you going to get the money?

Don't worry, I'll get it.

Where?

Somewhere.

Where?

I said don't worry about it.

Snapping on each light they pass, she follows him from the dining room to the living room, to the front door, their house getting brighter and brighter as they move through it, a cab honking now on the darkened street below. Turning, Murphy tries to keep his right hand on his wife's shoulder while he says, look everything's going to be all right. Go back to bed and *don't worry about it*. She pushes his hand from her shoulder and waits until he reaches the bottom of the stairs before she screams: you really got even with me didn't you!

When Murphy turns to answer, the door slams in his face.

When he gets to the Veterans Hospital, Murphy hands over his billfold, change, car keys. They take off his clothes, put him in a smock, stand him in a corner, lay him on a table, stick their fingers up his ass and decide, after three hours of vision and revision, that his appendix is going to burst if they don't remove it immediately, so they shave his stomach, groin, thighs, put him on a stretcher, wheel him into bright, white Ward C 32 R, lay him out on a bed and give him three hours to twist, turn, fear for his life.

Oh dear right smack across the ward from Murphy lies Dan Daneen 73 Years Old *oh dear* his name and age stenciled across a stiff, dishonored shard of cardboard adhesive-taped to the bile green wall above his bed *oh dear* which is not a bed at all *oh dear* but a coffin, an aluminum mesh cage into which they have slammed him in a maze of plastic tubes rammed up his penis, wrists and nostrils *oh dear* they have devised gloves for him *oh dear* canvas ping-pong paddles or pancakes within which he is unable to move his fingers *oh dear* making it damned near impossible for him to pick the plastic tubing out of his penis, nostrils and wrists *oh dear* after 73 years Dan Daneen has become no more or less than the public annunciation of his pain *oh dear*.

Like garage doors sliding open in the distance, the roll and boom of Murphy's bowels warns him that his time is near. Dan Daneen warns him too. Over and over again, he moans *oh dear, oh dear*. Listening to him, Murphy thinks of his night and wife, their party, fight, marriage. Between each *oh dear, oh dear,* Murphy tightens down on his teeth and pain, knowing as he does that the differences between himself and his wife are inevitable, will reoccur and reoccur within a system so raw and closed that neither of them will ever break out of it, ever understand whether they should pick up the phone or let the phone sit, go to the store or not go to the store, have a party or not have a party, double up their fists or simply slap each other across the face.

Stopping there, Murphy's gone only so far as to know he can go just a little further. So he admits that, more than anything else, what he's just thought about his wife and marriage is admissible. He'll tell the world. Standing tall among his friends, he'll tell them exactly what he and his wife will say and do to each other once they've all finished their beer and left nothing but the empties for them to scream amidst. With nothing to hide, he'll stand there and admit that if he didn't have his wife and marriage to torture over, he wouldn't know what to do.

Into that lie, Dan Daneen begins to cough. Murphy looks across the ward. The old man's head is shaved, his mouth is open, his feet thrash at the bottom of his bed. He chokes, strangles, reddens, keens.

Sitting up, struggling with his sheets, Murphy stares at Dan Daneen's open mouth and curses it. As he struggles from his bed, Murphy knows how carefully he's been trying not to remember what he's just been reminded of. As his bare feet touch the floor, Murphy prays that he will not have to admit what he has never admitted to anyone before, what he has done, god damn it, every time he hasn't had anything else better to do.

Looking for help, stumbling in a bend down the hallway, Murphy swings his head back and forth and tells himself that more than perverse, his bedroom closet is habitual, more worthy of resolution than admission. He'll simply stop going there. He'll promise himself to stop going there, and he won't have to promise anybody else that he's going to stop going there. Nobody will ever have to know that he's had a problem that's nobody else's business but his own, a bedroom closet he's had to squat and hide in every week or so or he wouldn't know what to do.

Bent almost double with pain, Murphy falls into the straight-backed chair in front of the nurse's desk. Breathing once he says, *that old man. The one across from me. I think he's choking.*

Laying a blond hand on his shoulder, she says, *I'll take care of it, you wait right here.*

Laid out and gliding below a sheet so cold he can't feel it, Murphy is certain that the operating room is moving toward him, not him toward it. Holding tight to the sides of the stretcher, he opens his eyes and the ceiling rushes past him. Below his feet and above his head, the attendants, gowned in ice green cotton, make a conversation that scrapes on and off like a dentist's drill. Closing his eyes as they enter an elevator, Murphy bears down and tries to contain his bedroom closet as certainly as he has contained his brawl with his wife, as certainly as he is containing the pain in his side. But it won't be contained. His bedroom closet admits and depicts itself on the slick dark screen of his tight-shut eyes. He sees himself stop at the top of a flight of stairs that still squawk and echo with his weight. Closing a last door behind himself, he snaps off the bedroom light and pauses only long enough to know how deliberately he pulled the blinds across the windows hours before. The light is golden, the ironing board opened, the pillows soft, the doorknobs burnished, the unmade bed slashed with a yellow blanket. The air is small, stale, used. As the lock snaps shut behind him, Murphy hooks his eyes to the left and right. Running his fingers across the door behind him, his heart slams against his ribs, squirrels scurry in a sudden rush across the rafters, Murphy passes with a swish of doors into the ice green precincts of the operating room.

Cold, frightened, he opens his eyes and tells himself that more than ugly, his usage of his bedroom closet is private. And since nobody has ever caught him at it, there's no reason to let them start now. No, the first thing he's got to do is to get through this operation, pass through the sodium pentothal without blabbing his mouth, without admitting his bedroom closet to anybody but himself.

Abruptly, that resolve is interrupted by the diamond of the operating lamp. An anesthetist leans into its light and says *how do you feel?* Startled, Murphy looks into the glinting rims of his eyeglasses and says, *fine I think.*

As it protrudes from his forearm, the needle casts no shadow. Nor does the anesthetist who is trying to puncture a vein with the tip of it. Even as he probes, Murphy is certain that the anesthetist is not going to find a vein until the third try. Beneath the sheet, Murphy feels almost invisible with defiance. As he looks at the needle in his arm, he finds himself thinking *let it get worse, let it get worse.* Out of the corner of his eye, he almost welcomes the hurry that's going on around him, the ice green ring of attendants bent on giving him much more help than he needs, perhaps even more than he can stand. Midway through the third injection, he begins to feel proud of the roll of his vein beneath the needle. It's not until the anesthetist mutters *I think we're going to get it this time* that Murphy remembers the silence he must maintain, the bedroom closet that he must not mention to anybody. And at the precise last moment when the needle gouges a vein, when the anesthetist breathes and says *there,* Murphy remembers too that he's forgotten to ask if Dan Daneen's all right. But afraid he's somehow too late, that his question would be confusing and that he wouldn't be awake for an answer, he doesn't ask it. Over and over he prays only that someone else will keep his mouth shut when he himself cannot.

Nothing as former as himself can contain Murphy's first fair

share of the sodium pentothal of this world. It ruptures a vein
so central and meager that

> ape-neck Murphy, child of
> scorn, slips upstairs and

into his wife's underwear. Closing the closet door behind him, he
squats and thinking of his wife as

> an empty overcoat, Murphy watches
> her get laid, fucked, raped, by the
> first 25 guys that come along, Murphy's
> head swaying back and forth amid his
> wife's silken dresses, Murphy gur-
> gling *hump her hard, god damn it, the*
> *bitch loves it*

again and again the bells of Murphy's orgasm shudder, but
little comes of such

> divorce, Murphy thinks, is not the
> word for it. The cock in my hand
> is caught in my throat

he chokes, and crashing past the silk linings of raincoats, Murphy
bursts from the closet.

With the care and acuity of a suicide, he avoids the mirror.
Coughing, he wipes his knuckles on the bedspread, takes off his
wife's frilly lace panties, girds himself in joyless Jockey underwear,
the corduroy Levi's of another brawl. Stuffing the panties into the
toe of an overshoe, he slams down the stairs, beats his stained
right fist on the kitchen table and tries to start a fight: I deserve
and demand a little privacy, he screams, and I'm going to get it
by god if I have to get it over your dead body

> hanging in his closet, the dumb
> glow-coat of masturbation staining
> the floor

then his wife grabs a butcher knife and shakes it in front of Murphy's face: I'm sick of your insanity, she screams, I can't stand it anymore. I'm going to take this butcher knife and I'm going to cut my throat from ear to ear

> Murphy grins into the teeth of his
> wife's corpse

then turning to her he screams: let me help you cut your throat, let me help you! Twisting away from him, she clatters up the stairs, and when he hears her fall onto the bed, Murphy falls to the floor, beats it once with his fist, once with his head.

Abject, migraine, his head rattles with his wife's sobs, rings with the chink of a tin shovel against concrete. Standing up, Murphy looks out the window and thinking of his son as a 4-year-old relic of his wrecked marriage, he whispers *Michael I love you*

> the atrophied valves of the
> heart expand and contract
> against the knuckles and
> thumbs of masturbation

Michael lifts his toy shovel. Striking it against the sidewalk he sings: *Old MacDonald had a farm* and Murphy bursts from the house.

Lifting his son onto his shoulders, he whispers: come on Michael boy, let's get the hell out of here, your mother's on a rampage

> up in the bedroom I've con-
> signed her to suicide, the
> benign kiss of the butcher
> knife

his wife raps three times on the bedroom window ledge, and pressing her fists to the screen she screams: you son of a bitch where are you taking my son?

Away from you.

No you're not.
Watch me.
I'll call the police.
Call them, call them
> I beg their attention, your
> rage, these trees that shake,
> sparkle, separate us step by
> step
Murphy steals away to Jesus.

What is Jesus?
Jesus is a parenthesis; a worn point of peace and punctuation
in a marriage of ice
> cream bars and screams; Old Mac-
> Donald on the cross; the nail,
> the bone, the pop of the cock,
> the squeak of Jesus in the
> marrow of Murphy and Michael
as they move across St. Matthew's lawn, stopping neither to kneel
nor to search for the key to the car, striding boldly instead through
the big double doors of a church not two blocks away from Murphy's closet.

Taking a place in the foremost pew, Murphy lifts Michael
from his shoulders, kisses him on the forehead, promises him an
ice-cream bar for just a moment's quiet
> with Jesus as obdurate moderator
> Murphy prays: good wife forgive me
> my closet as I forgive you your
> party and our friends, the bald
> musicians of my paranoia. Look
> down, sweet lady, the butcher knife

has fallen from your hand; penitent
and foregone
I return now to face the questions I can't answer.

Where have you been and where is Michael?
Michael is playing and I have been to church.
Are you drunk?
No.
But you've been drinking.
A little.
Where's the bottle?
From his coat pocket, Murphy draws a half-pint of tequila,
from his wife surprise and awe the
roar of her eyelids trying to close
put it away, she says. Give it to me. *Please* don't drink any more.
To your health
Murphy thinks, is a circular toast.
Tipping up the bottle, he drinks instead to a moment of pure
cactus, those small pandemoniums of throat by which he has
come to endure his own repetitions.
Stop it, she says. You'll go crazy again! You'll hit doors and
you'll threaten me!
No I won't. I came up here to apologize
to rehearse for the thousandth time
the impossibility of divorce, that
cold amputation I debate and debate
looking down at the butcher knife, Murphy promises not to hit
any more doors. I'm through threatening you, he says.
Give me the bottle then.
Not until you talk to me.
Talk to you! What do you think I've been trying to do

> all afternoon long, Murphy thinks,
> she has been trying to talk to me,
> trying to dissuade me from my closet,
> that stale joke by which I repeat and
> repeat myself

look, he says, I'm sorry I sulked around upstairs all afternoon. Let's talk.

About what?

About divorce

> the wet lace panties I stuffed so
> carefully into the toe of an overshoe

Murphy tips up the bottle and his wife screams: stop it! You don't want to talk, you want to show off!

I don't.

You do! Pretty soon you'll start slapping your forehead and moaning about how you feel trapped. Then you'll tell me how much you love your son and you'll start crying. Before I know it you'll be out in the alley with Michael on your shoulders, heading at a dead run for the god damned Catholic church!

Her predictions

> Murphy thinks, impell me not toward
> the church, but toward tequila, the
> fumes, nostrils and bolt holes of my
> fury

Oh stop it you phony! You make me sick! If you really wanted to talk, you wouldn't drink.

Drunk, Murphy walks to the closet door: do you see this?

She closes her eyes.

This wood is you. The way you rant at me so flat and thin.

Stop it!

Smashing his fist into the closet door

> Murphy shatters the surface of his
> masturbation

and his wife whispers: beautiful! That's beautiful!

Yes, Murphy screams, and if you weren't such a bitch, I wouldn't have done it!

Oh you'd have done it, she whispers, you'd have done it!

Bolting from the bedroom, Murphy charges down the stairs, lands with a leap right back where he started from: come on Michael boy, he says, let's get the hell out of here.

Where are we going Dad?

I don't know boy. Maybe we ought to blow down to
       Hernando, Mississippi, or through the
       hushed double doors of bright, white
       Ward C 32 R

Where Murphy finds no one but 73-year-old Dan Daneen, alone and systematized by plastic tubing so transparent anyone can see what's going on, what trouble he's gotten himself into, how close Dan Daneen has come to a very personal, yet public discovery.

Glancing over his shoulder, Murphy walks up to Dan Daneen's bed. Smiling, he reaches through the tubes and pats old Dan on the shoulder. He says, *I know you're too weak to talk, but I just wanted to come by to explain why I didn't ask about how you were getting along.* But just before he's finished with his lie, Murphy stops to look into Dan Daneen's eyes. And as he does, he knows he can't stop talking now, that he's going to say more than he should, that he has come this far just so he can go a little further.

Tugging gently on the tube that's rammed into Dan Daneen's right nostril, he says, *now listen there's just one thing I want to tell you. Neither of us has to admit more than he wants to. It's only right that we can keep certain things to ourselves.* But as Dan Daneen's eyes open white to what he's saying, Murphy tugs so hard on the tube, it jumps out into his hand. Shaking it in front of Dan Daneen's face, he knows that he has got to go just a little further, be just a little more insistent. *Look, we've all got things we don't want made public,* he says. *That's all I'm trying to say.*

When Dan Daneen's mouth opens and begins to fill with bile, Murphy leans down and whispers, *look I'm sorry you're dying, but if you promise never to do it again, I won't say a word to anybody. I'll take out all these tubes and forget all about it. You can go back home and not a word will be said to anyone.*

When Dan Daneen waves his canvas ping-pong paddles and gurgles *oh dear,* Murphy begins to pull all the tubes out of him. Yet as he rips the tubes away, Dan Daneen's *oh dear* amplifies and repeats itself until it overtakes and contains even the echo of Murphy's wife's high resolve: *I'm going to kill myself. I really am this time you son of a bitch. I'm going to kill myself.*

Clapping both hands over his ears, Murphy turns to a ward hung thick with swaying overcoats and raincoats, a bedroom closet within which he has repeated and repeated himself, Murphy stuffing his wife's lace panties into overshoe after overshoe. Now the overshoes begin to kick and stomp. Kneeling in the middle of them, pressing his hands to his ears, Murphy tries to make them stop. But they won't. He screams for help, but there's no one else who knows how much help he needs, there's no place else to hide, nothing better to do than look to the bed on which his wife lies with eyes tight shut and a butcher knife held at arm's length above her chest.

Awakening for the second time, Murphy recognizes the recovery room he failed to recognize before. Looking down at the six-inch stitch of piano wire in his side, he is glad that he has needed as much help as they have given him.

Then a hand begins to pat his knee. Murphy looks up into his wife's face and she is smiling. She squeezes his knee and says, *don't worry you're all right. Everything's going to be all right, everything's going to be just fine again.*

Then, though he's absolutely uncertain of what he's going to be able to do or say next, Murphy raises himself on one elbow and whispers: *not if I can help it, god damn it, not if I can help it.*

Murphy in Missouri

1

STRANGE mortgage. Tolling quiet. Murphy was playing house in hell again. Molly's hairpins glittered against the sheet, her hair fanned out over the pillow.

Next to the bed there was a straight-backed chair. A package of rubbers was nailed to it with a crooked spike of sunlight.

2

At 6 A.M. on Monday morning Murphy was sitting in the Labor Hall, staring at spittoons and old American Legion magazines, waiting for a summer job. Then somebody called out his name and half an hour later he lifted a 40-pound cement block with a bang to the floor of a scaffold and the examination of his conscience began.

Murphy had failed in the borrowed farmhouse with Molly and now with the sun glinting off the white limestone above him, he could admit it. Between Molly's uplifted knees he had faltered and faltered and now his teeth were grinding, there was sweat in his eyes, the palms of his hands were being cut on the edges of cement block after cement block, but he was picking them up and putting them down and he had found a place that was proper to his rage and humiliation.

Whoopee. He worked with a frenzied old wino name of Fred,

who had the ears of a bat and the chest bones of a bat. Fred screamed around with white saliva caked on his mouth and didn't remind Murphy in the least of pressing his closed eyes against Molly's breasts, every surface of her body a promise that had been made to him so long ago that Murphy couldn't spoil it now with his softness. He pressed against her, he told her that he loved her, and each time that he said it he got softer and softer, the willows flicking against the windows, pigeons stuttering and clucking across the floor of the attic above them, Fred screeching, screaming and flailing his bat's arms up and down, all tendons and pale bones with no bicep at all. Yet with his piebald bat's face tight with worry, Fred would hurry Murphy into slick blue corners and tell him to hand cement blocks to him, when from the floor overhead the red acetylene of the welders' torches was bursting and sizzling on the concrete deck around them. But Fred's skin didn't seem to burn and he didn't seem to care about the acetylene dribbling off his bony shoulders. So Murphy would cringe and lift and it didn't remind him at all of pressing against Molly in that squeaking beige bed when after a while he refused even to open his eyes, Murphy pressing and pressing and Fred running and running until just before noon, he almost nudged Murphy off the hoist they were unloading on the fourth floor. Murphy whispered *shit* and set a block down so hard it broke in half. Fred looked at him and said, "Boy, I believe you'd fuck up a wet dream if you got the chance." Looking into Fred's watery, unflinching eyes, Murphy tried to remember what Molly looked like. When he couldn't, he grabbed Fred's pale arm and shook it. He said, "You don't know what you're talking about old man. You'd better shut your mouth."

But Fred didn't shut his mouth. All afternoon he chattered and he hurried Murphy, the sound of Fred's high-pitched bitching driving Murphy straight into a tavern after work, Murphy drinking shot after shot of tequila, determined now to see Molly even sooner than he'd promised, buying a crazy, cortisone-colored hard hat from the foreman, smoking three black cigars, stumbling home after dark to the apprehensions and announcements of his 4-year-old son, Michael. "Daddy," he said, "I think Momma's sick." Plopping the hard hat down on Michael's head, Murphy hugged him and carried him up the stairs. His wife was sitting in the bathtub, her head hung down and her hair streaming into the steaming water. Murphy reeked of tequila and his nose was stuffed with concrete dust. When he bent over and asked her what was the matter, she said "Ahhh" three times.

Three days later, she was stretched out on an operating table, having a tumor removed from her bladder.

3

Postoperative hugs and whispers. Murphy hung around his wife's hospital bed as nice and fuddled as a new father. Both of her roommates were old ladies with cancer and sons killed in the Korean War. Their distraught daughters would rush in from time to time and try to keep the old ladies in bed while they reported the fatal illnesses of other and still younger daughters in Texas and Detroit.

Outside, the big purple rain clouds piled up, sent sheet after sheet of rain against the windows and Murphy was sure he would not work the next day.

So he said to his wife: "Sure I'll work tomorrow. I'm in with the foreman. I'll work inside. He knows I need the money."

That afternoon they held hands and talked about how they'd been treating each other. Murphy bought his wife a chocolate malted, and they promised to try to help and love each other in spite of their complications and problems. Her urine was siphoning into a plastic bag at the side of the bed, and she seemed brave and distinct in her new madras bathrobe. Time and again he squeezed her hand and told her the biopsy would come back from the lab negative. Of course the tumor couldn't be cancerous. She shouldn't even consider it. She was much too young.

He kissed his wife's hand at 4 Sunday afternoon, called Molly from the phone booth in the lobby of the hospital and told her he was on his way. Then he checked with Michael's babysitter and ten minutes later he took off for Des Moines through squalls of blue Iowa rain.

4

Rife with wives on brave vacations, the motel parking lot filled at dusk with rainbows and nervous fathers unloading the luggage racks of side-swiped Chevrolets from Minnesota, Utah, Nebraska. With arms drawn and shoulder sockets squeaking, skinny sons in T-shirts carried suitcases up and down the staircases. Flamingo daughters in shorts and pincurls opened folding cots and large, stained sackfuls of hamburgers-to-go. Then as the parking lot lights snapped on, Molly stepped from amid the honking vans and station wagons into Murphy's rented room and bed, a thrashing, chafing, hour-long struggle that tossed the blankets and twisted the sheets, closed Murphy's eyes on a single certainty. Over and over he whispered, "I want to be *in* you Molly," and each time he repeated his words, he was sure only that his softness was rubbing his wife's tumor wrong, that if he kept at it that tumor would bloom and flower in the lab and on her bladder, Murphy finally rolling away from Molly, telling her it wasn't any good, and Molly whispering, "It's all right. I understand."

"What do you understand?"

"That you think I'm a child. A little girl you can't be responsible for."

Shaking his head, Murphy reached out, snapped a ripped package of rubbers from the nightstand, found the lie that saved him.

Crumpling the foil in his fist he said, "This is why it isn't any good. I hate these things. They separate and humiliate us."

Even before it was over, the horns of the parking lot began to honk and bleat against Murphy's speech, Molly to touch his cheek and turn his face toward her. When Murphy looked away she said: "You don't want to make me pregnant do you?"

Murphy shook his head. "No I don't. I want to make decent love to you though. And I can't with one of these on."

On the strength of that lie, Murphy pulled Molly toward him, began at the same time to think about making her pregnant. He thought about ripping the rubber off and pinning her to the bed. She would squirm whispering: "You don't want to make me pregnant do you?" and Murphy would say: "Yes I want to make you pregnant," then with a thrust and shudder he'd engender a fix he couldn't get out of, strike a blow that would devastate his wife and marriage.

Just loud enough to hear himself think, Murphy began to whisper: "Molly I'm going to make you pregnant." Again and again he whispered it until he began to feel hard and sure about what Molly could give him and he could take from her for the first time in her life. Then, for the first time in either of their lives, sheathed and steady Murphy moved into Molly.

Humility and gratitude. He moved up and deeper into her, and the difference between Molly and his wife was thunderstruck, diametric, clutching; again and again Murphy went as deep as Molly did. When she began to moan "Oh," Murphy felt as if by length alone he could drive back and undo every tumor, marriage or woman he had ever made before her.

5

Two days and 150 miles later, his wife didn't have cancer and all summer long Murphy lifted concrete blocks onto ringing scaffolding and paid Molly's bus fare to come see him.

Broad Sunday afternoons they lay under a friend's skylight, in a friend's low bed, breathed the air conditioning, ate Dexamyl and drank tequila. While pigeons wheeled across the skylight, Murphy pulled his mouth off Molly's mouth and told her that he loved her, that he wanted to *keep on* loving her, that he didn't want to stop just to go to Kansas come September, just to take a job he didn't care about, with no one out there to love or live for.

Monday mornings dawned resonant with jackhammers and disbelief. Full of his wife's bacon, eggs and blueberry pie, Murphy would lean and yawn in the cool caves of the unfinished fourth floor. He'd smoke a cigar and look down on razor-backed Fred scurrying in the muddy arroyo below him, racing amid the ghostly boa constrictors the tires of the wheelbarrows left behind. Then the air compressors would rack on and Murphy could feel, but couldn't believe, the waltz of his and Molly's skeletons as they fleshed and coalesced while they whispered "love" and the Sunday sun sank to the squawk of the bed, faded to the blue hiss of her bus leaving for Des Moines.

6

Now Murphy stands at the poolside of a darkened Holiday Inn in Columbia, Missouri, and looks out over the suitcases and luggage racks of the republic. He thinks of his last desperate promises to take Molly to Mexico. He thinks of a brave new station wagon with her fragrant combs and sunglasses spread across the top of the dashboard. Roaring semitrailer trucks might blare their horns and bright lights at them, but behind the tinted glass, amid the air conditioning, she would be asleep with her head on Murphy's lap, and he would stroke moist wisps of hair from the corners of her mouth and together they would drive to that serene southern border in less than two days.

Molly.

Murphy raises the pint of tequila to his lips, and his anger is as amnesiac as it is drunken. He lowers the bottle, puts the tips of his fingers to his chin, but no matter how quietly he stands, he cannot remember what Molly looks like.

That loss of memory turns him on his heel. With raw tequila sloshing on the toes of his shoes, he heads toward room 126 and his hands remember yesterday. At first he sat on the front porch, drank beer, jiggled Michael on his knees and declined his wife's invitation to help the truck driver load the furniture onto the moving van. But then the driver offered him $2.50 an hour, and now Murphy can feel the sharp wrought-iron chairs and slick refrigerator in his hands and would like to raise them over his head and smash them through the motel door. He stops in front of it and in his 2 A.M. guts he can feel that moving van whining toward Kansas and he would like to throw out a fist and stop it.

He fits the key into the bright red door of room 126, pushes and thinks he can't do it. He can't go to Kansas just to prove that he can't take Kansas, just to break down under that truck and the solid job that awaits him in Manhattan.

The stage, the altar. Murphy steps onto the motel room carpet, drinks and looks. He knows that with a single shout he could have the lights on, he could have the floor strewn with shredded Kleenex and his wife propped up and rocking, moaning: "You can't be serious. A 19-year-old girl. Have you gone mad? You can't leave us this way. We're your family."

And she would be right and his son would be sitting up rubbing the sleep out of his eyes and Murphy can't do that to either of them. So while his family sleeps, he drinks and wanders in their midst, looking at them.

He stops first in front of his wife, who lies curled as if she were expecting her pillow at any moment to sputter and catch fire. Murphy smooths her hair and lifts the blanket to her hand. When she clutches it to her throat, he knows he had no right to touch her. Drinking, he moves to his son, who sleeps as if his father had never driven to Des Moines.

Because it is the closest he can now come to Molly, Murphy must caress and displace that lie. Putting down his bottle of tequila, he sweeps up his sleeping son, steals out the door and down the steps. He stops at poolside, holding him against both suicide and abduction under a bright dome of Missouri stars.

Making the most he can of his grip and judgment, Murphy walks to the edge of the pool and stares at the sign Deep End. And because he doesn't need to be reminded, he looks into the water and is reminded of driving to Des Moines: the wobbly yellow squabbles of Fred and his wife's cancerous roommates as they hopped from the back seat to the front and twisted the rearview mirror and stared into each other's throats; the rain hitting the car like bedsheets filled with lightning and the fluted grills of semi trucks; his wife's biopsy hanging like an ulcerous albatross around his neck. Then the sky cracking open and Des Moines diaphanous with rainbows, tequila and Molly in full wine regalia knocking at his door and in bed her thighs opening exactly as wide as the question of his wife's cancer until they finally closed on him and annulled everything and one that came before them in a benign fusion of pink flesh and flaring bone, white flesh and fusing bone.

Now he opens his eyes, presses his son's sweet skull against his own, and because Murphy must put the Deep End of his memory in words, he whispers: "I love you, Michael boy," and his son sleeps on as if that assertion need never have been made.

Holding cheekbone against cheekbone, he feels the slow marrow of his son's sleep growing between himself and Molly. But as he holds him there so surely above the water, there is nothing short of murder that he can do about it.

Murphy turns from the pool, and because there is something mean and desperate in him that wants his wife to wake and find them gone, he hurries with his son toward darkened room 126.

Murphy's Misogyny

BEGIN with Murphy on a sentient binge at the hinge of his first 4th of July alone. It's Sunday afternoon, all the taverns and the liquor stores are closed. This is Kansas. Sour and stalwart, Murphy stands on the football field surrounded by a hooting hangover and the adroit playmates of his late twenties. They are playing *touch*. At the snap of the ball, tombstones erupt and Murphy's flat on his back on his dim living room floor, two ten-pound dumbells in his hands, making the elbow motions of health. In his bathroom, in his bathtub, a Baptist minister's 18-year-old daughter sits in six inches of tepid water, the shower curtain pulled around her, a candle flickering on the soap tray, a cello churning and squawking between her knees. Straining to hear the sound of Annie's cello, Murphy moves down the long, battleship gray corridor. It's a strange building, built long and low like a ship, with portholes instead of windows. In the air there's a scent of box lunches, mayonnaise, rancid butter, a smell of band directors and music majors, a bellowing of bassoons, oboes, French horns, bass fiddles. Murphy peers into each porthole that he passes. His progress is slow. Past pianist, harpsichordist, violinist and trumpeter, Murphy moves in a dream of ships, ocean liners. Beneath his feet, he feels the floor pitch and roll, imagines the whole Fine Arts Center caught at midnight in a storm in the middle of a pan-Kansas passage, its portholes twinkling against a tinkling of pianos, a sigh of violins, the grasses and wheat fields swaying and parting before its plowing hull, the big smokestacks belching jet black smoke, the deck trembling and bucking now as Murphy arrives at the end of the corridor, the last porthole into which he can peer.

Pressing his nose to the glass, he looks into the soundproof cubicle, the smoke-choked practice room. Annie is sitting in a straight-backed chair in front of a full-length mirror, a cello between her knees, a cigarette in her mouth. Curling up into her eyes, the smoke pinches her face, knits her brows. On the piano bench beside an overflowing ashtray, she has emptied the contents of her purse. From the tilt and angle of her profile, Murphy knows she knows he's looking in at her. But she doesn't let on. Stubbing out her cigarette, she picks up the bow. Placing it upon the strings, she bends forward, her hair falling around her face, the fingertips of her left hand pressing and whitening against the bow strings, her intensity and concentration complete, a committed and serious cellist about to make an attack on Bach. Then, because he knows she wants him to, Murphy surprises her with a knock on the door. Her smile is bright, quick. As she turns, Murphy can see that she has been expecting him, that her face is perfectly made-up. Unlocking the door, she says oh good. You're here. Sit down, I want you to listen to this.

Obedient, claustrophobic, Murphy pushes his chair into the corner so he can't be seen from the corridor. The air is dense with cigarette smoke, mascara, eyeliner, resin. There are two empty cups of Coke on the floor, cigarette butts, candy wrappers, bits of tobacco floating in the melted ice. Murphy lowers his eyes and Annie begins to play. But only for an instant. Because she's made, as always, a mistake. Sitting up in her chair, pulling it closer to the point where the end pin of her cello is anchored to a crack in the tile floor, she whispers *shit* and shakes her head, trying somehow to erase the mistake with her flying hair. Then she begins again. Only, of course, to make another mistake. But this time she scrapes and descends into it, completely losing her way, the cello moaning and complaining, the bow sawing back and forth across the strings, resin flicking up into the smoke-filled air. As she plays, Murphy raises his eyes and envies her. Because as the music gets worse, the melody more and more completely lost, she seems to lose herself in her playing, seems free and relieved of it, her head bending down and her hair falling into the strings, Murphy himself suddenly the only one responsible for the noise she's making, the flat, off-key, singsong squawk of her cello settling in a hot ball of embarrassment at the very center of his gut.

Looking up and out the porthole onto the prairie and parking lot, Murphy watches the Shriners' Drum and Bugle Corps march uphill against the wind, their tassels, feathers and visors flickering in the sun, their fierce director gesticulating and shaking his fist, the glint of his teeth turning Murphy's thoughts toward Annie's teachers, the mild, attentive, bespectacled bastards who, having misled and encouraged her some $4\frac{1}{2}$ years in her playing, are asking now that she perform before assembled faculty, student body and guests, a graduation recital. Which is, of course, a requirement. And they must insist upon it.

Upstairs in a soundproof, portholed practice room, Murphy can hear them insisting upon it. Four and a half years of congratulating, coddling and prodding conclude now in a single cruelty. Through Annie's wailing and calamitous cello, they will ram a selection each from Bach, Brahms, Mozart and Schubert, a grinding, groaning succession of sounds designed to plunge Annie again and again into Murphy's bathtub. Against the squeal of a cello and a splashing of soapy water, Murphy anticipates Annie's endless bathing. As her graduation recital approaches, she will spend less and less time in the practice room, more and more time in the bathtub. On the soap tray a candle will gutter,

95

flicker. In the rose-scented water Annie will soak and soap herself, rising in towel after towel to squat monkey-style on the edge of the tub. Bending forward, she'll study and manicure her toenails. Her hair will be in rollers, at the corner of her mouth she'll show a tip of tongue. As she squats there it will be very important to get each toenail clipped just right, the quality of her Bach, Brahms, Mozart and Schubert dependent somehow on the length and curvature of each toenail that she clips. Through the steam and perfume, transparent paper dress patterns will float and wilt. Against the suck and rumble of the plumbing, Murphy will hear the whir of her mother's sewing machine. Down there in Shawnee, Oklahoma, the needles will flash in the velvet and taffeta. But for Murphy the dress will be a surprise. He will not see it until he sees it at the recital. And as that time approaches, Annie's bathing will become more fevered. So that on the night of the recital, with Murphy squirming uncomfortable in a freshly pressed suit, it will be as if Annie steps directly from the bathroom onto the stage, the bathroom door slamming to a smattering of applause, a rush of steam and bath salts filling the recital hall, Annie being applauded for the shimmer of her dress and the sheen of her hair, somewhere below her full-length dress and patent leather shoes her toenails communicating their perfect curvature and shape to the audience, filling them with admiration, awe, the practice room filling now with a smoke-choked silence, Murphy looking up to confront a question Annie seems to be asking almost incessantly these days: well, she says, what do you think of it?

Of what?

The Bach.

It was fine.

As good as the Brahms and Mozart?

Sure.

Oh *good*. Now the Schubert. Won't you *please* listen to the Schubert? Just once more?

Once more, once more, Annie's Schubert poses the question, provides the opportunity of Mexico. And Murphy must go there again and again. It is an endless trip, an ancient complaint, a mistake Murphy must repeat as often, it seems, as Annie must repeat her Bach, Brahms, Mozart, Schubert. Sitting with his chair shoved up against the practice room wall, battered by the shrieks and sadness of her Schubert, Murphy wonders what would make Annie a good cellist. Would her teachers have to take her bow and break it, seize her cello and smash it against the wall, take all of her cosmetics, dresses, and burn them, tell her to return naked to her childhood, to begin again with the humming of some simple tune, explain finally when all else failed that she had chosen to be a musician because she knew she would fail at it, that the only way she could have her Bach, Brahms, Mozart and Schubert was to stay away from them? No, it wouldn't work. Because as he watches her bow bounce and wobble on the strings, Murphy knows that since they are all she can make, Annie's fallen in love with her mistakes, just as, though he knows it to be wrong and even cruel, Murphy has fallen in love with Mexico and its memory, believes that if he recalls it often enough, he will discover why he went there with Annie in the first place, why he is sitting now in a smoke-choked practice room, listening to her butcher Schubert.

Mexico begins, as always, with the evidence of Mexico. Murphy goes there so that going there can be held against him. By his wife. In sunstruck, burnt-out July. Under the crow-slashed

skies, as always, of the Veterans Cemetery. Darkly tanned and
dressed in tight, white Levi's, her hair done up sun-bleached in
a blue bandanna, Murphy's wife walks in front of him, picking
up rocks, chunks of white limestone, from the winding driveway,
tossing them as hard as she can at each pine tree that they pass.
Her accuracy is uncanny and funny. But noon tequila won't let
it be. Nor will the gardenias and diarrhea of the Hotel Chicago in
Guadalajara let it be. Under Murphy's feet the white driveway
of the Veterans Cemetery curves off brilliant through Texas into
Mexico and back again, its sides piled high with fly-thick, truck-
killed cattle and horses, Mexico nothing more or less than a big,
wobbly, Dexamyl-crazed circle returning Murphy again and
again to Kansas, a confession he must try over and over to make,
his wife getting a little bit sick, she says, of talking about *Mexico,
Mexico, Mexico,* Murphy shaking his head and insisting that
they've got to talk about it, his wife turning toward him now to
whisper *why?*

Because there's something I haven't told you about it.

What?

When I went down there in June, I wasn't alone.

What do you mean you weren't alone?

I took Annie down there with me.

The words, when he speaks them, squawk like Annie's cello.
Seizing it by the throat, Murphy raises it above his head. Against
screech after screech of Schubert, he smashes it down again and
again, flecks of resin flying up from his wife's sun-bleached hair,
the knees of her tight, white Levi's slamming time after time to
the ground, her blue bandanna filling with the blood and bone
bits of divorce, remarriage and childbirth, the words *I took Annie
down there with me* confirming and completing his wife's next
marriage, the twin daughters, honking station wagons, Volks-
wagens, Ford Family Vans and baby grand pianos her red-
bearded second husband will in the next three years provide for

her, his wife's spinning looms and strawberry fields, her city homes and farm homes bursting snow white from the burnt-out grass of the Veterans Cemetery, her goats, pigeons and ponies screaming in the falling snow as she turns now toward Murphy and says *what did you say?*

I said I took Annie down there with me.

Do you mean, his wife says, you took that weasel-faced little bitch down to Mexico with you?

Murphy nods and Annie smiles. Wizened and weasel-faced, she squats in the crow-slashed shadows, sawing at her cello. It is a stone cello and Annie is a tiny pine-green granite angel grinding inside the petals and vermiculations of tombstone and obelisk, her face tightening, crumbling and flaking with each note she plays, her Schubert blending with the two-throated, mineral-thick horn of a huge station wagon that advances now along the white driveway of the Veterans Cemetery. Inside it a red-bearded man grins at the red-haired twin daughters to which, in less than a year and a half now, Murphy's wife will give birth. Looking beyond their father's shoulders, they raise their weasel pink palms in the air, call through the grinding granite of Annie's Schubert for their *mama, mama, mama.*

Against such impatience, Murphy's wife curses both Mexico and the *weasel-faced little bitch* Murphy took down there with him, wants to know why *god damn it* he did it.

I already told you why.

No you didn't.

Yes I did: I was tense and tired; I needed to get away.

From me?

No.

From what then?

Even before he says *everything,* Murphy's answer excepts Annie. But Murphy answers anyway. He says *everything* and his

99

wife says *shit,* trips with a flicker of white limestone, a resolve upon which Mexico seems to rest and insist: to prove he's gone there once, Murphy must go there twice, add to the injury of June the insult now of August. Looking down at his wife's bright, white Levi's, Murphy says *wait a minute,* but she waits a good deal longer. For hours she seems frozen in front of him, trying to believe what Murphy is about to tell her. There is a chunk of white limestone gripped in her right fist and her hesitation seems somehow bridal. Along the white driveway of the Veterans Cemetery a station wagon advances and Murphy's wife frowns now and asks him what the hell he wants.

I want to tell you something.

What?

June's not all. I'm going back down there again.

What do you mean?

I mean I'm going to take Annie back down to Mexico with me in August.

Murphy's words, when he speaks them, seem to shake crows not only from the pine trees of the Veterans Cemetery, but from the pine trees of Durango too: black wings flap and beat against a vow his wife makes him repeat and repeat, the words *Annie* and *Mexico* and *August* pulling from Murphy a plan of borrowed cars and borrowed money, drawing through his wife's white teeth a disbelief that turns finally into anger. She whispers *damn* and Murphy feels the battered Volkswagen explode. Crows wheel black above the bodies of Murphy and Annie, her cello shattered, her long hair soaked in blood, her life snuffed out at sweet 18, the exact and damning fact that makes his wife stop Murphy now to ask: how old is this little bitch anyway?

I don't know.

Yes you do.

No I don't.

I'll bet I know someone who does.

Murphy looks at her and his wife says: do her *mommy* and *daddy* know she's going down to god damned Mexico?

Yes.

With you?

No.

Whispering *Jesus,* his wife turns, shakes her head and says: do you know what's going to happen? You're going to screw around and lose your job. You're going to get in a wreck down there, there's going to be a big god damned scandal and you're going to lose your job.

Murphy shakes his head and she screams: well I'll tell you something! I'm not going to let it happen; I'm not going to let you do it! I'm going home and I'm going to call that little bitch's parents, and if that doesn't work, I'm going to call your boss and the dean and the president of the god damned school!

But even as she makes her threats, they betray her: take her no farther than the far side of the Veterans Cemetery, a lace-iron bench toward which Murphy follows her for a last interrogation, final grilling: you know don't you, she says, what I'll do if you take her down there with you again?

Yes.

I'll leave you, I'll divorce you.

Yes.

Is that what you want?

Yes.

Even as she turns away from him, Murphy is tempted to stop her. But he doesn't. A station wagon advances along the white driveway of the Veterans Cemetery, and Mexico is an arc best described not by Schubert but by Gershwin: rattling the dashboard of the battered Volkswagen, "Rhapsody in Blue" and "Slaughter on 10th Avenue" drive Murphy past crazed Mexico

City taxicabs through Texas back to Kansas and a departure he hopes right now is final: *god damn,* he thinks as his wife disappears amid the sunlight and the pine bows, *that was easy, that was easy.*

But Mexico is not easy. Nor is August easy either.

Murphy's Xmas

1

MURPHY's drunk on the bright verge of still another Christmas and a car door slams. Then he's out in the headlights and in bed waking up the next afternoon with Annie kissing his crucified right fist. It's blue and swollen, and when he tries to move it, it tingles, it chimes and Annie says, How did you hurt your hand? Did you hit somebody?

Murphy waits while that question fades on her mouth, then the room glitters and he sniffs the old fractured acid of remorse asking: Was I sick?

Yes.

Where?

On the floor. And you fell out of bed twice. It was so terrible I don't think I could stand it if it happened again promise me you won't get drunk anymore, Glover had to teach both of your classes this morning you frighten me when you're this way and you've lost so much weight you should have seen yourself last night lying naked on the floor like something from a concentration camp in your own vomit you were so white you were blue

is the color of Annie's eyes as Murphy sinks into the stars and splinters of the sheets with her, making love to her and begging her forgiveness which she gives and gives until Murphy can feel her shy skeleton waltzing away with his in a fit of ribbons, the bursting bouquets of a Christmas they are going to spend apart and

bright the next morning they rise in sweet sorrow to part for Christmas; she to her parents' home in Missouri, he to haunted Illinois.

Murphy holds her head in his hands and whispers: I can't leave you. I won't be able to sleep. I know I won't. I'll get sick. I need you Annie.

She squeezes his shoulders, kisses his cheeks and tells him he can do it. It's only for two weeks. Good-bye. And be careful. Driving.

The door slams, the windows rattle and Annie walking through the snow is no bigger than her cello which she holds to her shoulder, a suitcase bangs against her left knee and the door opens and there's Glover jangling the keys of his Volkswagen, offering again to drive Murphy's family into Illinois for him.

Stricken by swerving visions of his son strewn across the wet December roadside, his toys and intestines glistening under the wheels of semi trucks, Murphy says no, he will drive and as he takes the proffered keys, Glover says: Is Annie gone already? I was supposed to give her a cello lesson before she left

then he leaves, the door slams and Murphy hates him, his Byronesque limp through the snow, his cello and his Volkswagen and sobriety. Rubbing his right fist, Murphy goes to the kitchen and drains a can of beer. Then he packs his bag and lights out for his abandoned home.

2

Now the trunks are tied down and the Volkswagen is over-laden and they roll out of Kansas into Missouri with the big wind knocking them all over the road while vigilant Murphy fights the wheel and grins at the feather touches of his 5-year-old son, who kisses his neck and romps in the back seat, ready for Christmas.

In Mexico, Missouri, his wife looks at his swollen right fist and says: Tsk-tsk. You haven't grown up yet have you. Who did you hit this time?

Into the face of her challenge, Murphy blows blue cigarette smoke.

When they cross the Mighty Mississippi at Hannibal, she looks up at the old, well-kept houses, pats her swollen stomach and says: Maybe I could come here to live, to have my baby.

Murphy's son rushes into the crack of her voice. And he doesn't stop asking him to come back and be his daddy again until Murphy takes Dexamyl to keep awake and it is dark and his son is asleep and the Volkswagen hops and shudders over the flat mauve stretches of Illinois.

At Springfield, where they stop to take on gas, the fluorescent light of the filling station is like the clap of a blue hand across the face. Murphy's son wakes and his wife says: This is where President Lincoln lived and is buried.

Where?

In a tomb. Out there.

She points a finger past his nose and Murphy makes a promise he knows he can't keep: I know what. Do you want to hear a poem, Michael?

With his son at the back of his neck all snug in a car that he should never have presumed to borrow, he drives through Springfield trying to remember "When Lilacs Last in the Dooryard Bloom'd." But he can't get past the first stanza. Three times he repeats "O powerful western fallen star," and then goes on in prose about the coffin moving across the country with the pomp of the inloop'd flags, through cities draped in black until his son is asleep again and

that coffin becomes his wife's womb and from deep in its copious satin Murphy hears the shy warble of the fetus: *you are my father, you are my father,* the throat bleeds, the song bubbles. Murphy is afraid enough to fight. He looks at his wife and remembers the wily sunlight of conception, the last time he made love to her amid the lace iron and miniature American flags of the Veterans Cemetery (it's the quietest place I know to talk, she said) while the crows slipped across the sun like blue razor blades and the chatter of their divorce sprang up around them

stone and pine, lilac and star, the cedars dusk and dim: *well it's final then, we're definitely going to get a divorce?* Murphy said *yes,* for good? *yes* and his wife caught him by the hip as he turned away *well it's almost dark now so why don't we just lie down and fuck once more for old time's sake here on the grass come on there are pine needles and they're soft*

Did you take your pill?

Yes

Ok, but no strings attached and

3½ months later Murphy is informed that he is going to be a father again and again, hurray, whoopee now

Murphy drives across slippery Illinois hearing a carol of death until the singer so shy becomes a child he will never hold or know, and the sweet chant of its breath gets caught in the whine of the tires as he imagines holding the child and naming it and kissing it, until it falls asleep on his shoulder — *how could you have tricked me this way? how could you have done it?*

That question keeps exploding behind Murphy's eyes, and when they hit his wife's hometown, he stops the car in front of a tavern and says: I can't do it.

What?

Face your parents.

He gets out: I'll wait here. Come back when you're unloaded.

His wife says *wait a minute,* and Murphy slams the door. He walks under the glittering Budweiser sign and she screams: I can't drive. I don't even know how to get this thing in reverse . . .

Push down.

Child!

Murphy hovers over the car: *I'm not a child!* and the motor roars, and the gears grind, and the Volkswagen hops and is dead. A red light flashes on in the middle of the speedometer and Murphy turns to the wakening face of 5-year-old Michael: Are we at Grandma's yet Daddy?

He slams his swollen right fist into his left palm: Yes we are!

Then he gets in and takes the wheel. And he drives them all the way home.

But he doesn't stop there. Murphy roars northwest out of Illinois into Iowa in search of friends and gin he can't find. Then he bangs back across the Mississippi, cuts down the heart of Illinois, and holes up in the YMCA in his wife's hometown, within visiting distance of his son.

Whom he loves and doesn't see. He keeps telling himself: *I think I'll surprise Michael and take him to the park this afternoon,* then he races down to the gym to run in circles and spit against the walls. He sits in the steam room, watches the clock and slaps his stomach, which is flat, but on the blink. To ease his pain, he drinks milk and eats cottage cheese and yogurt and calls Annie long distance in Missouri: God I love you and miss your body Annie I haven't slept for two days

and she says: Guess what?

What?

Glover was through town and gave me a cello lesson, he's a great guy his gifts are stunning and relentless, he limps off to take your classes when you're too drunk to stand up in the morning — his hair is scrubbed, his skin cherubic, his wrists are opal and delicate; right now Murphy would like to seize them and break them off. Instead he says: Is he still in town?

Who?

Glover.

Heavens no, he just stopped through for about two hours are you all right?

Yes. Listen Annie I love you

Murphy slams the phone down and bounds back upstairs to his room in the YMCA to sit alone while his cottage cheese and yogurt cartons fill up with snow on the window ledge and he imagines Annie back in their rooms in Kansas. When she walks across the floor her heels ring against the walls and every morning Murphy hears her before he sees her standing at the stove, her hair dark, her earrings silver, her robe wine, her thighs so cool, and the pearl flick of her tongue is like a beak when she kisses him

Murphy tastes unbelievable mint and blood and

imagines Glover limping across the floor of the living room with two glasses of gin in his hands. The betrayal is dazzling and quick. Bending under Glover's tongue, Annie whispers *no, no,* and as she goes down in their bed, her fingers make star-shaped wrinkles in the sheets

Murphy slams his fist down on his YMCA windowsill. Then popping them like white bullwhips over his head, he stuffs his towels and clothes into his bag, and lights out of there on lustrous Highway 47. The night is prodigal, the inane angels of the radio squawk out their thousand songs of Christmas and return. Bearing down on the wheel, Murphy murders the memory of Annie and Glover with the memory of his father, whom he has betrayed to old age, the stars and stripes of the U.S. Mail.

Composing them on the back of his American Legion 40 *and* 8 stationery, Murphy's father sends quick notes By Air to his grandson saying: I was feeling pretty low x until I got the pictures you drew for me Michael boy x then I bucked up x God bless you x I miss you x give my love to your daddy x who

unblessed and rocking in the slick crescents of Dexamyl and fatigue, is on his way home for still another Christmas. Now as he drives, he notes the dim absence of birds on the telephone lines, and thinking of the happy crows that Michael draws with smiles in their beaks, Murphy sees his father stumbling under the sign of the cross, crossing himself again and again on the forehead and lips, crossing himself on his tie clasp, wandering in a listless daze across the front lawn with a rake in his hands, not knowing whether to clean the gutter along the street or pray for his own son, who has sunk so low out in Kansas.

It is just dawning when Murphy breaks into the mauve and white outskirts of his dear dirty Decatur where billboards and *Newport* girls in turquoise are crowned by the bursting golden crosses of Murphy's high school then

he's home. Pulled up and stopped in his own driveway. And sitting there with his hands crossed in his lap he feels agog like a Buddhistic time bomb about to go off, about to splinter and explode inside the dry sleep of his parents, the tears will smoulder, the braying angels of insomnia will shatter around the childless Christmas tree, there will be a fire, it will sputter and run up the walls and be Murphy's fault. Sitting there he feels hearts beginning to pump in the palms of his hands and he doesn't want to let anybody die

as he knocks on the dry oaken door of his parents' home and is welcomed with open arms and the sun rising behind his back

Inside the sockets of his mother's eyes, there are mauve circles and they have had the living room walls painted turquoise. Murphy blinks, shakes his father's hand, and his mother leads him into the kitchen.

There he drinks milk, eats cottage cheese and kisses his mother's hands. She cries and wants him to eat a big breakfast. With tears in her eyes, she offers him bacon, eggs, cornbread, coffee, butter-chunk sweet rolls and Brazil nuts. When Murphy shakes his head she says: I think you're making the biggest mistake of your life, I think you'll live to regret it. Patricia is a lovely girl, you have a wonderful son and another child on the way. Isn't there any hope of you getting back together? I pray night and day and can't get little Michael off my mind. What's ever going to happen to him and the new child? Oh I wish I were twenty years younger

After breakfast they go shopping, and for his Christmas present Murphy picks out three packs of stainless steel razor blades and a pair of black oxford basketball shoes. Then he slips off for a work-out at his high school gym. The basketball team is practicing and Murphy runs in wide circles around them, not bothering a soul.

Left to himself that afternoon, he drinks rum and eggnog and plays with the remote controls of the color television set. Then he roams the house and neighborhood and everything has changed. The sheets of his bed are blue. On the walls, where once there were newspaper photographs of himself in high school basketball uniform, there are now purple paintings of Jesus Christ kneeling on rocks in the Garden of Gethsemane. Every place he looks, in corniced frames of diminishing size, there are color photographs of Murphy in tight-collared military attire. As he looks, the photographs get smaller and smaller and there is always a snub-nosed statue of St. Francis of Assisi standing there, to measure himself by.

Up and down the block, birds bang in and out of bird feeders. The withering neighbors have put up fences within fences within fences. Half-drunk, Murphy keeps hitting the wrong switches and floodlights glare from the roof of the garage and light up the whole backyard. All night long his father keeps paying the encroaching negro carolers not to sing. Finally Murphy gets up from the sofa, and smiling, announces that he's going out. Taking his rum and eggnog with him, he sits in the Volkswagen and drinks until 3 o'clock in the morning. Then he gets out, vomits on the curb and goes back inside

Where his mother is awake in a nightgown of shriveled violet, with yellow spears of wheat sewn into the shoulders like crossstaves of static lightning about to go off and how

will Murphy hold her when she stops him on the carpet outside his bedroom door to tell him that she loves him, that he will always be her son no matter what happens she is so sorry that he had to leave his wife and children for

a mere girl, it is unbelievable that

in his hands her small skull buzzes and even before she mentions the fact of Annie, Murphy is holding Annie's skull in his hands and the sinking wings of his mother's sweet shoulders are Annie's shoulders in his mother's nightgown sinking: What are you talking about?

That girl you're living with. She called tonight

on Christmas Eve

Murphy hears the old familiar bells of his father's fury gonging

Your father answered, he was furious

Mother I'm not living with anyone

Michael I know you are

then the small lightning of her nightgown begins to strike across her shoulders and she is sobbing against his throat and Murphy is in bed holding his lie like a sheet up to his chin: Mother I told you I'm not living with anyone

Stroking his leg through the blankets, she disregards the crocked insomnia of his eyes, and makes him promise to try to sleep: Do you promise now?

Yes Mother, I promise

and she leaves him sleepless between the blue sheets with Christ kneeling on the wall, the scent of his mother's handcream on the back of his neck and he hears her alone in her room coughing like a wife he has lost at last and picking at her rosary beads all night long

There is no sleep

or peace on earth. But with the muzzy dawn Murphy rises and goes to church with his parents. In the choir loft, the organs shudder; in his pew Murphy shivers and sniffs the contrition of Christmastide. All around him the faithful kneel in candle smoke and pray; all day long Murphy kneels and shuffles around trying to get Annie *long distance,* trying to tell her *never to call him at home again.* Then at 7 P.M. the phone rings and Murphy's simmering 70-year-old father answers it hissing: Long distance, for you

By the time Murphy hangs up, his father is dizzy. He staggers through the rooms slamming doors while Murphy's mother follows him whispering: Mike your blood pressure, your blood pressure

Then in the living room they face each other: The bitch! Calling here on Christmas Day! The little bitch!

Murphy turns to his mother and says, *I'm leaving* and his father spins him by the shoulder: You're not leaving, *I* am!

They both leave. Murphy by the back, his father by the front. Storm doors slam, crucifixes rattle on the walls. Murphy's father rounds the corner and screams: Come back here!

His voice is higher than Murphy has ever heard it, and the

wind pulls at their clothes while they walk toward each other, his father in a slanting stagger, his overcoat too big for him, his eyes filled with tears.

I'm an old man. I'm dying. You won't see me again. Go back to your family, don't abandon your son.

Murphy reaches for his shoulder and says *Dad I can't* and his father slaps his hand away

Michael Murphy. You have a son named *Michael Murphy* and you tell me you can't go back to him?

Murphy lifts his hand and starts to speak, but his father screams: *Phony!* You're a phon*eee*, do you hear me?

They are at the door and Murphy's mother, in grief and her nightgown, pulls them in. His father stumbles to the wall and hits it: You phony. You ought to be in Vietnam!

Murphy's laughter is curdled and relieved. He slaps his hands together and screams: That's it, that's it!

Then he spins and bolts toward the back door, with his mother screaming: Michael! Where are you going?

To Vietnam, god damn it! To Vietnam

Which isn't far. 150 miles north. From a motel room deep in her own hometown, Murphy calls his wife and when he asks her to come over she says: Why *should* I come over?

You know why. I'm going out of my mind.

Be my guest.

Click

She opens the door during half-time of a TV football game and neither of them says a word as their clothes fly in slurred arcs onto the bed. Then standing naked in front of her, Murphy hunches up with holy quietude and smiles and breathes as he holds a glass of gin and tonic to her lips and she drinks and smiles as the lime skin nudges her teeth and she nods when she's had enough. While her mouth is still cool, Murphy kisses her tongue and gums and wants to push the bed against the wall and then to drive all the other guests to insomniac rack and ruin by humping and banging the bed with wet good health against the wall all afternoon but

his wife is sunk in an older despair. She runs her fingers up the vapid stack of Murphy's spine and says: You *are* handsome. I love to touch you.

Bare-chested Murphy turns on it, and the quick trick of her flattery gets them into bed, where to the pelvic thud of the innerspring she sucks on the spare skin of his collarbone and says: Tell me that you love me. You don't have to mean it. Just say it . . .

Murphy would like to but he can't. Both memory and flesh legislate against him. He looks down, and like painted furniture his wife's ribs now seem chipped by a thousand kicks; when he takes them in his mouth, her nipples taste as tight and deprived as walnuts; within the pregnant strop of her stomach against his, Murphy can feel the delicate strophes of Annie's waist, and moving like a pale liar before his wife's bared teeth, he remembers the beginning of the end of their marriage; the masks, mirrors and carrots that began to sprout around their bed like a bitter, 2 A.M. Victory garden, one that Murphy had planted all by himself and was going to pick and shake in his wife's face on the sparkling, sacrosanct morning that he left for good and ever. Caught in the dowdy mosaics of their bedroom mirror, they would get down on their hands and knees and as the orange joke of a carrot disappeared between her legs, his wife would turn and ask, *who are you?* and Murphy would smile down from behind his mask and say: *who are you?* Then his smile would rot in his opened mouth, and Murphy *became* his impersonations; he played and moaned within an adultery so hypothetical it stunk and smoked the bedroom ceiling up like the induced death of love between them *Harder, Oh Harder* now Murphy and his father are standing outside the motel room window looking in at Murphy's marriage like peeping toms and his father is ordering Murphy back into the bed but Murphy resists and all of his reasons are rosy and shrill like a schoolboy he screams: *I wouldn't swap Annie for anybody, do you hear me, not anybody* and his father, in tears and death, screams: *Not for your son? Not for Michael Murphy? I'm*

   Coming

and Murphy opens his eyes to endure his wife's orgasm like a slap across the face *Oh Thank You God, Oh Thank You.*

Thanking her with whispers and pecks about the neck and ears, Murphy sweeps his wife out into the brittle December afternoon and bright the next morning he picks up his son to take him home, 150 miles south, to his grandmother. Michael's raucous teeth glitter in the rearview mirror of the VW, and as they rattle into Decatur, Murphy loves him so much, he can't stop or share him with anybody just yet: I know what Michael. Do you want to go to the zoo before we go to Grandma's? Yes

he does. Right now. And Murphy, full of grins and flapdoodle, takes him there. He buys Michael a bag of popcorn, and as he goes back to the car to flick off the headlights, he turns to see the popcorn falling in white, jerky sprays among the ducks and geese.

The whole pause at the zoo is that way: spendthrift, inaugural and loving. Murphy squats and shows Michael how to feed the steaming billy goat with his bare hands. He flinches and giggles at the pink pluck of his lips, then they race over to look through the windows at the pacing leopards. Bare-handed and standing there, Murphy wonders how he would defend his son against a leopard. He can feel his fists and forearms being ripped away, but also he can feel his son escaping into the dusk and dim of the elm trees that surround the zoo.

Then he gets zany and amid giggles and protests, Murphy drives the borrowed VW up over the curb and through the park to Grandmother's house they go with the radio blaring: help I need somebody's help then

suddenly it's darker and cooler and their smiles are whiter when the subject changes like a slap across the face to

Michael's dreams. Five years old in a fatherless house, he sleeps alone and dreams of

snow. Murphy pulls him into the front seat, sets him on his lap and turns off the radio. Holding him too tight, he says: what kind of snow Michael?

You know. The kind that falls.

What do you dream?

That it's covering me up.

Then Michael begins to cry and says: I want somebody to sleep with me tonight and tomorrow night. I want *you* to sleep with me Daddy.

Murphy does. Three nights they stay in his parents' house and Murphy sleeps between the blue sheets while Michael sucks his thumb and urinates the first night against Murphy's leg, giving him the chance to be patient father loving his son

he carries him to the bathroom with sure avowals and tender kisses: That's all right Michael boy, Dad will take care of you

Always?

Always

and Murphy's mother is there in her nightgown in the stark light of the bedroom changing the sheets, putting down towels, kissing her grandson, wishing she were twenty years younger

In the lilac morning, quick with clouds and sunlight, Murphy and his mother and son go uptown. Standing in front of laughing mirrors in the Buster Brown Shoe Store, Murphy and Michael grow fat and skinny and tall and short together, then go to see Pinnochio not in the belly of a whale

but in the outer space of sure death and forgiveness, they eat silver sno-cones and Murphy is finally able to eat steak while his father roams through the rooms presenting his grandson with a plastic pistol on the barrel of which an assassin's scope has been mounted.

Compounding that armament with love, he displays, on the last afternoon, Murphy's basketball clippings. Spreading them out for his grandson on the bed, he whispers, smiles and gloats until 5-year-old Michael can't help himself. He walks over to Murphy and says: Grandpa says you were a great basketball player and played on TV

is that right Daddy?

That's right Michael, then they

are leaving. Clasping his toys to him, Michael cries pained and formal tears. Murphy stands on the curb, the wind in his eyes, and the apologies are yet to be made. Overhead the streetlight clangs and they are standing on the same corner where Murphy used to sit under the streetlight at night on the orange fire hydrant twirling his rosary beads like a black propeller over his head waiting for his parents to come home and light up the dark rooms with their voices and cigarettes then

he would see their headlights coming up the street and he would rise and put away his rosary beads to greet them now

he takes off his gloves and puts out his right hand to his father and says: Dad, I'm sorry.

When his apology cracks the air, his mother begins to cry. Grateful for that cue, his father takes his hand and says Good-bye, good luck, God bless you

3

Out there in Kansas the next afternoon, under a sere and benedictory sun, Murphy's Christmas comes to an end. He tools west away from home and the holidays, southwest toward the snaggled conclusion of still another New Year. His family rides

in a swarm of shredded Kleenex, Cracker Jack, and terror re-
ferred

is terror refined: like the crucial envoy of his grandfather,
Michael, sweet assassin, holds his plastic pistol to the base of
Murphy's skull and says: Daddy? Why don't you come back
and be my daddy?

Terse and perspirate, Murphy's wife takes a swipe at the pistol,
but Michael moves out of her reach, and keeping it trained on
the back of his father's skull, he repeats his question: Why don't
you come back Daddy?

Before he can think or excuse himself, Murphy says, *Because.*
Because why?

Because Mommy and I fight.

You're not fighting now.

In tears and on her knees, Murphy's wife lunges into the back
seat and disarms her son. But he begins to cry and find his ulti-
matum: Daddy

I'm too shy to have a new daddy, I want you to be my daddy,
and if you won't come back and be my daddy

I'm going to kill you.

The moment of his threat is considered. And then it is foregone. Out of his fist and index finger, Michael makes a pistol
and a patricide: Bang, bang, bang

you're dead Daddy

you're dead

Coffin that passes through lanes and streets, Volkswagen that
blows and rattles under the new snow's perpetual clang, here,
Murphy hands over his sprig of lilac and return, his modicum
of rage and disbelief.

Certain that his son's aim was shy and hypothetical, he stops
the Volkswagen in front of his apartment, flicks off the headlights, slams the door and hears the

dual squawk of tuned and funereal cellos

their notes curdle the snow, splinter the windows with a welcome so baroque and sepulchral, Murphy can't stand it. Roaring toward the door, he imagines Annie and Glover sitting on stiff-backed chairs, their cellos between their legs, their innocence arranged by Bach, certified by

the diagonal churn of their bows on string, the spiny octagons of their music stands, the opal bone and nylon of Annie's knees. Murphy rattles the door with his fist, and for a moment their music needles his rage, then squeaks to a stop. In turquoise slacks and sweater, with a smile brimful of tears and teeth so bright, Annie throws open the door and how

will Murphy return her kiss, while blurred in the corner of his eye, Glover scurries, gathering up his cello and his music: *Happy New Year did the car run all right* he takes the proffered keys and

guilty of nothing but his embarrassment

he says *don't mention it* as he leaves, slams out the door, and

left in the rattled vacuum of that departure, Murphy has no one to beat up or murder, no one on whom to avenge his Christmas; he is left with only the echo of the music, a suspicion founded on nothing but a cherub's limp and hustle through the chiming snow.

In bed, Annie is a sweet new anatomy of hope and extinction. She kisses him, the *Newport* flood of her hair gets in his eyes and Murphy cracks an elegiac and necessary joke: *Annie you'll never leave me for Glover will you?* She tells him not to be silly then

Murphy kisses her, and in a rush of flesh and new avowals, he puts everything into his lovemaking but his

heart

which hangs unbelievable and dead in his ribs, all shot to smithereens by Michael.

Outside the new snow falls and inside it is over. Annie is asleep in his arms and Murphy lies sleepless on a numb and chiming cross of his own making. On the walls there are no praying Christs, the turquoise Gethsemanes of Decatur are gone forever. The clock drones, the womb whirs, the shy trill of his wife's gestation comes to Murphy through the pines like Michael calling to him: *Sleep with me tonight and tomorrow night Daddy* the cradle's eloquence depends on pain, it is sewn in lilacs and shocks of wheat. Shy charlatan, Murphy sneaks up to it and in a room full of white, white sunlight, he looks in at his newborn child, and cannot look away or kid himself, his fatherhood is the fatherhood

of cottage cheese, the retreating footprints of snow and yogurt up his father's spine, the borrowed Volkswagen that will never run out of gas or plastic pistols. Then the dry bells of the furnace begin to hiss against Murphy's ankles, and he hears the whistling pines, the clangorous tombstones of the Veterans Cemetery. Flapping their arms like downed angels in the middle of winter, Murphy and Annie make love and forgive each other until their ears and eyesockets fill up with snow

then Michael stands over them, takes aim at Murphy and
makes his final declaration: Bang
bang, bang
you're dead Daddy
you're dead

4

And for the first time in his life, Murphy lies there and knows it.